THE
PROPHET
CALLS

The Prophet Calls

Melanie Sumrow

 YELLOW JACKET

This is a work of fiction. Any references to historical events, real people, or real places are used fictitiously. Other names, characters, places, and events are products of the author's imagination, and any resemblance to actual events or places or persons, living or dead, is entirely coincidental.

YELLOW JACKET
an imprint of Bonnier Publishing USA

251 Park Avenue South, New York, NY 10010

Copyright © 2018 by Melanie Sumrow

All rights reserved, including the right of reproduction in whole or in part in any form.

Yellow Jacket is a trademark of Bonnier Publishing USA, and associated colophon is a trademark of Bonnier Publishing USA.

Manufactured in the United States of America BVG 1018

First Edition

10 9 8 7 6 5 4 3 2 1

Library of Congress Cataloging-in-Publication Data is available upon request.

ISBN 978-1-4998-0755-4

yellowjacketreads.com

bonnierpublishingusa.com

To Shane & Madeline,
with all my heart

1.

"Let's play apocalypse!" my cousin yells.

In the shade of the general store, my three mothers shake their heads in unison.

Sweat creeps down my back. It's so hot already. I wish I could strip off the long underwear beneath my ankle-length dress, but the Prophet says we must always wear our sacred underwear if we want to survive the real apocalypse.

Several of the kids squeal, "We're gonna die!" I have twenty-one brothers and sisters and about eighty cousins. Most of them scatter and duck behind the piñon trees.

My younger sister tugs on my hand. "Gentry, let's hide before the government comes." A few strands of Amy's light-blond hair have already escaped her braid.

I shift between my feet, fighting the urge to run off with her. "I can't."

"But you're my partner in crime," she says, mimicking the words I've used on her so many times. When I don't budge, she pushes her thick glasses up the bridge of her nose. "You always play."

I shade my eyes from the midmorning sun with my hand as I try to figure out how to explain. She's right; I *always* play. The problem is, it's my thirteenth birthday, and I'm not supposed to play anymore.

I thought I'd wake up and find someone different in the mirror today: a grown-up Gentry. But I'm still wearing the same old prairie dress with the patched rip in the sleeve. I have the same freckles across my cheeks and the same red hair in a long braid down my back. I look and feel the same as I did yesterday and the day before. I still want to play.

Tanner smacks my arm with a grin. "You two better run, or else." He wiggles his eyebrows. My older brother is sixteen and likes to pretend he's an evil government agent.

Channing Snell bumbles up behind him, his dark hair flopping across his forehead. There's a fading bruise on the side of his neck. "What's the holdup?" he asks. He's the same age as me, but he's still allowed to play.

"You know I'm not supposed to," I say, pushing my sleeves up to my elbows. My gaze moves between the huddles of older girls in pastel dresses. That's where I'm supposed to be now.

It takes me a second to find my sister Meryl, sitting alone on a wooden bench. She reads a spiral-bound copy of *Pronouncements of the Prophet.* With her golden hair in a fancy braid and large blue eyes, she resembles our mother more than any of us. Meryl is my most beautiful sister. She makes the best green chile stew and can recite all of the Prophet's revelations from memory.

Meryl shares the same mother as Tanner, Amy, Baby Bill, and me, but she's nothing like us—she's a total rule-follower. And very, very good at getting me into trouble. I'd say they switched her at the hospital, but we don't have one.

She looks up from her reading and automatically zeros in on me. Meryl points to my arms. I quickly shove my sleeves down to my wrists before she has a chance to rat me out to Mother.

"Since when do you do anything you're supposed to?" Tanner asks as he tugs at his buttoned-up collar.

Channing gives a knowing laugh. "Come on, Gentry. One more time?"

Kids streak past, yelling about explosions and gunfire. Our baby brother wails in Mother's arms. Meryl rushes over to dig inside my brother's diaper bag and soon pulls out a bottle. She hands it to our mother.

"Please, *please* play with us," Amy says in a drawn-out voice.

I look over at our other mothers. Father's first wife, Mother Lenora, approaches Mother Dee. While they chat, Mother

Lenora slides her hand around the circumference of Mother Dee's pregnant belly. No doubt Mother Lenora is rattling off about how it's a wife's duty to bless her husband. She's kind of a know-it-all that way. In all ways.

Our mother starts to feed Baby Bill.

"You're not scared, are you?" Tanner asks with a grin.

"Please," Amy says. "You find the best hiding places."

Meryl and our mothers are too busy to notice. Would it really hurt to play one more time? I turn to Amy. "Come on. I know just where to hide."

Amy giggles as we take off and run uphill, darting past the New Mexican scrub and sagebrush that litter the foothills surrounding us.

Behind us, I hear Channing counting to fifty.

"They're coming," Amy says, pretending a large army is after us. Some of the smaller children begin to cry.

Our shoes form clouds of dust as we zigzag between the junipers and yellow-flowering brush along the hillside. Amy sometimes has a hard time breathing, so I try to find a good hiding spot for her to catch her breath.

When we've gotten higher than everyone else, we duck behind an oversize lavender bush. We brush against it, and the flowers' sweet perfume fills the air.

I wipe the sweat from my forehead and peek beyond the

purple flowers. From up here, I can see past the concrete wall that surrounds our community and keeps the rest of the world out. I scan the scrub-covered hills and the Sangre de Cristo Mountains in the distance, trying to spot the nearest town, but it's no use. We're miles away.

Amy breathes heavy through her mouth. She points to a Mexican elder tree a few feet from us. "We could . . . climb it," she suggests, winded. Amy's the best tree climber I know—fast and sure-footed. But she's still out of breath.

"Let's stay where we are," I suggest, since no one's following us. Yet. I point to the blue and cloudless sky, whispering, "Bomber planes." My sister shivers. Maybe she's also imagining the dead bodies of some of our brothers and sisters scattered along the hillside after the government's planes drop missiles on all of us.

Downhill, our cousins pretend to aim cannons and shoot down the planes. A few of the boys act like airplanes and make crashing sounds. As God's chosen people, we'll have to defeat the government at the end of the world in order to bring about a thousand years of peace. I just hope I'm ready when the time comes.

"We're winning," Amy says, excited.

A black-tailed jackrabbit bounds out from behind a nearby bush, startling Amy and me. Its long, broad ears bob with each hop. "Rabbit," Amy screams and almost darts out from our hiding place to chase it.

I snag her skirt, keeping her hidden. "Not now. They'll see you."

From the base of the hill, the older boys begin to charge and yell, "Die!"

Between heavy breaths, Amy wheezes as she realizes she's given away our hiding spot. "What're we gonna do? The government agents are moving uphill."

My heart races with excitement. "Let's keep climbing."

"But they'll see us," Amy protests as I take off.

After a second, I realize I don't hear the pounding of my sister's shoes behind me. I turn and see she's fallen not far from the lavender bush. The boys have stopped midway to throw imaginary grenades at another group of kids. I lift the hem of my skirt and run downhill toward my sister.

Amy sits up, her face scrunched in pain, as I get to her. Red dirt covers the front of her yellow dress.

I drop to my knees and try to stay hidden. "You okay?"

She holds out her hand for me to see. It's bleeding a little from where she hit a small pointy rock. A tear runs down her dirty face. "I thought you were gonna leave me," she says, still winded.

"What?" With my thumb, I wipe her tear and smear away

the dirt on her cheek. "I could never leave you." I take the underside of my skirt and blot the blood from her hand.

My sister rubs her lips together like she's unsure.

"Never." I kiss my index finger and touch her cut softly. "Ever."

That brings a smile to her face.

"You sure you're okay?" I ask.

With a sniffle, Amy nods. I help her stand and brush the dirt off her dress as much as I can before Meryl or our mothers see it.

Below, some of my half brothers and sisters are starting to sneak away from their hiding places and form prayer circles at the foot of the hill. They link hands. After the real battle at the end of the world, we're supposed to gather here in Watchful or in Waiting, our sister community in Canada, to pray for God's deliverance.

Outside one of the prayer circles, Channing stumbles. He clutches his chest, pretending he's been hit, and drops to the ground.

If Amy and I can get to a circle without a government agent killing us first, we're saved.

"Gotcha," Tanner yells from a few feet away, making us both jump. He pretends to throw a grenade, but we dodge it and start the downhill run. Although holding Amy's hand slows us, I don't let go.

Suddenly, the prayer circles break apart. What are they doing? That's not how the game works.

My feet come to a sudden stop. Amy bangs into my back, nearly knocking me over.

"Ow," she says as she adjusts her glasses. "That hurt."

My muscles tense when I see him. The bishop of Watchful paces along the bottom of the hill. With a long neck and a beak-like nose, Uncle Max likes to strut around in his black suit kicking up dust. He's not really our uncle. He's one of the Prophet's brothers. We're supposed to call him "uncle" out of respect.

"Children!" Uncle Max screeches.

Tanner shrieks softly behind me. Once, I made the mistake of telling him Uncle Max reminds me of a vulture. Amy giggles.

I smack Tanner's arm to shush him before he gets us all into trouble.

"By the way," Tanner says under his breath. He axes our shoulder blades with the side of his hand. We flinch. "You just got the tomahawk. You're both dead."

Amy looks worried, but I shake my head and whisper, "It doesn't count since we had to stop in the middle of the game."

The concern leaves her face. "Yeah," she says a little too loud. Tanner smiles.

"Children!" the Vulture screams again.

Now he's looking at us. Me. I wipe my sweaty hands on my skirt.

His beady eyes narrow, and I hope he doesn't remember I'm thirteen today. The last girl he caught playing after she turned thirteen had to sit in his office and write *Obedience is the key to my salvation* one thousand times without food or bathroom breaks. And that was one of his easier punishments.

No one says a word as we wait for Uncle Max to speak. It's so quiet I can hear the drum of a hummingbird's wings flitting from flower to flower on a red-blooming salvia bush somewhere nearby.

Uncle Max finally turns in the direction of the meetinghouse. "It's time for service," he says. I can breathe again.

We merge in with the rest of the Prophet's followers at the base of the hill. Channing has already joined his brothers and sisters. My family, along with the hundreds of other residents of Watchful, funnels toward the meetinghouse. We're not supposed to talk. As we walk, we're supposed to think about all the sacrifices the Prophet is making for us. He's in prison in East Texas, far from Watchful. My parents won't tell me why, but Meryl says it's because the outsiders hate us.

Tanner elbows me in the ribs, but I don't dare cry out. I've already had a close call with the Vulture today. And once is enough for anybody.

When my brother doesn't get a rise out of me, he drops back in our family's moving cluster. He bumps around with some of our half brothers until he finally gets Kel to squeal. Amy and I chuckle.

Mother Lenora turns and glares at us. I bite the inside of my cheek to keep from laughing.

After a few minutes, we reach the large meetinghouse with its rust-colored stucco walls and flat roof. We move past the heavy wooden door into the darkened foyer. I shiver from the sudden coolness.

Out of nowhere, a hand with long, pale fingers grabs my arm. I gasp as my eyes adjust to see Uncle Max.

His face pinches as he releases me. "Disgraceful," he says. His breath smells sour. He points to my skirt. That's when I look down and see the two red dirt spots around my knees.

My heart bangs against my ribs. I'm caught.

Tanner's still goofing off as he walks through the door. Uncle Max snatches him, too. "Not so fast," he croons.

The dumb grin leaves Tanner's face.

"I must speak with *both* of you."

I stand, frozen.

My brother's gaze darts between Uncle Max and me for a clue as to what's going to happen next.

All I can think is now would be a really, *really* good time for the world to end.

2.

Uncle Max beckons us to follow him. I swallow hard as we move away from the stream of people entering the meetinghouse.

As soon as Tanner and I turn the corner, I spot the worn leather strap. It hangs from a rusted nail on the wall. The sight of the leather makes me shake.

Tanner's nervousness radiates off him. He's so uptight, his shoulders almost touch the bottom of his ears.

Uncle Max stops near a small window, just inches from the strap.

The meetinghouse door slams shut, making both Tanner and me jump.

From the sunlight coming through the window, I can see the painful-looking red bumps that run down the Vulture's long neck and disappear beneath his starched collar. Obsessed with neatness, he's shaved too close again. My stomach turns at the sight of a sore that oozed a drop of scarlet onto his white collar. His Adam's apple rises and falls as he swallows. "We have a problem."

I clench my hands, expecting the strap to come off the wall any second. Why did I have to play?

It's all I can do to keep from shoving my brother toward Uncle Max and making a run for it.

The only reason I don't is because I know I wouldn't get very far. Buckley, the red-faced goon, and his God Squad guard the meetinghouse during service with their guns. Once the door closes, no one gets in. No one gets out.

Uncle Max raises a pale, slender hand. I flinch. "The Prophet hasn't called."

Huh?

Tanner looks as stunned as I feel. "But he always calls," my brother mutters. "Eleven o'clock, Sunday morning."

"I'm aware, son." Uncle Max smooths the front of his suit jacket even though it's already perfect. "I need you two to stall."

Us?

"Stall?" Tanner repeats. His upper body relaxes a little. "How?"

Uncle Max flaps at us. "Conway said you could play your violins while we await the Prophet."

Butterflies fill my stomach. Sure, Tanner and I play together at home. But that's for our family. "We've never played in front of the whole community," I say. My voice comes out smaller than I'd like.

"Are you telling me your father has lied?"

"No," Tanner says. "We can do it."

My eyes go wide. No, we can't.

"Good," Uncle Max says with a nod. "Conway has already placed your instruments on the stage."

My stomach folds over on itself, squishing all the butterflies.

Uncle Max walks away from the window. "Don't make me wait too long."

When he's gone, I turn to my brother. "What's wrong with you? We can't play in front of all these people."

Tanner shrugs. "Why not?"

"For starters, they'll think we're worldly." Most people in our community don't have musical instruments. They think those kinds of things are a waste of money that would be better spent paying for the Prophet's lawyers, who are working day and night to get him out of prison.

My brother rolls his eyes. "Who cares what *they* think? Father thinks we can."

"But he has to think that. He's our father."

"It will make Mother so happy." He nudges my arm. "All of those hours and hours of practice."

"No fair." Mother's the best music teacher in the world. There's no telling how many hours she's worked with us, and it would make her so happy if we did well.

When I was little, Mother tried to teach me piano, but I wanted to be like Tanner and play the violin. He nears the prayer room, nervously picking his ear before smearing his finger across his pant leg. "So, I guess you're gonna tell Uncle Max we won't do it, then?"

"Fine," I say with a sigh. "One song."

Tanner points to my skirt. "You better dust that off first," he says and then smirks while giving his best Meryl impression, "A grown woman should never allow herself to get so dirty."

I shake my head. "Says the boy with earwax on his pants."

He ignores my insult and heads toward the prayer room. I quickly brush the dirt off my skirt and follow him through the replica of the Prophet's prison cell.

We all must experience what our lack of faith has done to the Prophet. So Uncle Max had a fake prison cell built. There's no way to get to the prayer room without passing through the musty space. It gives me the creeps. The windowless "cell" has bars from floor to ceiling with a dirty cot shoved against the wall. A single light bulb buzzes overhead. There's even a stainless-steel toilet in the corner. It doesn't actually work, though. One of my little brothers already tried it.

I squint at the natural light coming through the windows of the large prayer room. Uncle Max insists the women of the community keep the room spotless, and the whole place smells of pine disinfectant. My eyes burn from the fumes.

Across the length of the room, our community sits in long rows of metal folding chairs. Kids younger than eight years old sit on the floor near the stage up front. Uncle Max is on the stage, talking into the microphone. He explains how everyone is in for a real treat this morning.

As he gestures to the back of the room, heads turn. People stare at Tanner and me. My heart flip-flops as I search the faces for my family. They're in their usual spot in the center of the congregation.

Amy smiles and waves when she sees me. I quickly wave back. A few adults chuckle, making my face go hot.

My sister pats the seat next to her, showing me where to sit. I almost join her, but I hear Tanner's shoes thud across the carpeted stage. He walks past my violin case and is already pulling his instrument from its case. Uncle Max's eyes narrow. People mumble, and I force myself to move toward the front.

My feet feel heavy as I walk, as if sacks of flour are weighing them down. The chatter grows louder with each step. I hear fragments of my name.

When I finally reach the stage, Tanner has tuned his instrument. The Prophet glares at me from his massive portrait that hangs on the wall behind the stage. From the front row, the Prophet's eighteen-year-old son, Dirk, sits and stares at me along with everyone else.

My body's shaking as I turn to pick up my violin, which suddenly looks tiny in my hands. If only I'd gotten a full-size one for my birthday. I've grown so much in the last year; my old one is too small. It's harder to play now when my fingers are all cramped together.

I look from my violin and see the Prophet's portrait again, but now, it's even closer. A lump lands in my throat. I tuck my violin under my right arm and pull my bow from the case. Rosin dust flies from the horsehairs and tickles my nose. I sniffle and will myself not to sneeze on Uncle Max's stage. My trembling fingers fumble with the screw at the end of my bow until I finally get it to twist and tighten.

"Thank you, Uncle Max," Tanner announces. I have no idea what we're going to play. I meet my brother center stage and pluck the strings of my violin with my thumb to make sure they're in tune. The tip of my bow hangs against my long skirt, swinging between the folds.

Tanner lifts his instrument and addresses the congregation. "Our first hymn is 'Glorious Things Are Sung of Zion.'"

People shift in their seats. They're all watching us. From the back corner of the room, Channing gives us a thumbs-up. I feel sick.

Tanner nods toward the little kids and mouths to me, *Just look at Amy.*

Somehow, our sister is there, sitting right up front with the little kids. She must've moved when I had my back turned. Amy smiles and gives me a wink behind her thick glasses. Her confidence helps me relax. A little.

I bring my violin under my chin.

"G major," Tanner whispers, quickly reminding me of the key signature.

My bow touches the D string as we begin. Tanner plays the melody, and I play the harmony. We both pull long, smooth strokes across the strings. Sustained chords echo against the walls of the prayer room.

Halfway through the second verse, I hear Amy singing the lyrics like we do at home. I shake my head slightly. I don't want her to get into trouble. But she keeps going.

To my surprise, Uncle Max starts to sing with her. When we reach the third verse, other voices slowly seep in and join theirs. The knots in my neck loosen. We play a little bolder. By the end of the fourth verse, it sounds like everyone is singing, *"And we'll know as we are known."*

When we sound the last chord, Amy claps. She's the only one. I lower my violin and hold it against my body. Then, I notice the congregation smiling. The adults. The kids. Everyone. I don't remember seeing so many of God's chosen smiling without being ordered to do it first.

Tanner nods, acknowledging Amy's applause. I don't take a bow, because that would be prideful. But I can't help but feel proud. I smile instead.

Amy jumps to her feet, enthusiastically clapping above her head.

From the corner of my eye, I notice Dirk shift in his seat. He shoots my sister an icy glare.

My skin suddenly feels clammy. "Amy," I say under my breath, trying to make her stop. But she keeps going.

"Hey, retard," Dirk taunts.

I flinch. She stops clapping.

Dirk rises from his chair in the front row and hovers over Amy and the other kids. "I'm talking to you."

My hand clenches my bow so hard it nearly cuts my hand. It's not the first time someone has called her that awful name. Amy has Down syndrome, but that doesn't mean she's a retard or stupid or any of the other horrible things people say. Dirk is just mean. And, because he's the Prophet's son, he can get away with it—Dirk the Jerk.

At first, Amy seems shocked. She looks embarrassed. Her cheeks turn pink as she looks behind her.

"Yeah, stupid, I'm talking to you," he jeers.

I take a step forward. "Leave her alone." Several gasp as Tanner pulls me back into place. A girl's not supposed to talk back to a man, especially not the Prophet's son.

Dirk turns his scowl to me. "Your sister's so stupid she has to sit with the little kids now?"

Some of the boys in the audience chuckle. Technically, Amy's eleven and shouldn't be sitting up front anymore. Of course, *technically*, Dirk's face is as ugly as the east end of a horse headed west, but we still let him sit in the front row.

I shift forward. Tanner yanks on me once again. "Don't," he whispers.

Dirk lifts his chin as Amy lowers hers and pushes her fingers under her glasses to wipe the tears from her eyes.

"You're such a jerk," I say.

"Gentry. Elaine. Forrester," Father warns. Loud. So loud I can feel the boom of his voice inside my chest. He's standing now, too. His face is as red as our hair. Mother sits to his left. Her eyes fall to the pink carpet, and I know I've humiliated her.

I suddenly look down and away when I realize everyone's judging me.

"We'll discuss your punishment at home," Father says.

Punishment?

I glance up. But what about Amy? Who's going to speak up for her if I don't? If only I could tell Father none of this would've happened if *he* hadn't suggested we play for the congregation. That all I wanted was to sit next to Amy and remain anonymous.

Amy wades through the little kids to get to the side aisle. Dirk tries to trip her, but she manages to get past him and keeps going. He laughs, mocking her again.

"Do you have something to say for yourself?" Father asks me, even though it's not really a question.

Mother Lenora sits to his right. Her arms fold over her round body. Like she's enjoying this a little too much.

My jaw tightens.

When Amy reaches the center of the room, moans and groans rise from my half brothers and sisters as she bumps into them and hurries to climb over their legs and reach our mother.

"Sorry," I mumble.

A smug grin spreads across Dirk's face, but I'm not talking to him. I'm talking to my sister. *I'm sorry there are jerks in this world that don't see what a blessing you are.*

"How—how about another hymn?" Tanner suggests.

Dirk nods at Father, and they both take their seats.

From the stage, I can see Amy bury her face in Mother's

side. I bite my lip and place my violin under my chin, ready to get my mind on something—*anything*—else.

But Uncle Max touches the scroll on Tanner's instrument. "The Prophet calls," he announces.

"Thanks be to God," the crowd responds in a monotone voice.

Uncle Max suddenly looks annoyed that we're still onstage. "Put your instruments away," he tells Tanner and me. "Go to your seats."

We quickly place our violins in their cases. But as I descend the steps, Dirk snatches my left hand with his sweaty one. I manage to rip my fingers away and wipe them against my skirt. I glance at the nearest adult and then the next. But they act like they didn't see anything.

If any other boy had tried to take my hand, no fewer than ten adults would be pointing their fingers. Yet nobody says a word to the Prophet's son, even though he should know better. After all, his father's the one who preaches unmarried boys and girls risk death if they even *think* about touching.

I want to kill him myself for putting me in danger. But Tanner doesn't give me the chance. "Keep moving," he says as he hurries me up the aisle to the empty seats on our family's row and then traps me between Mother and him.

"All right," Uncle Max says into the telephone. "Everyone

is in place." He sets the phone onto a docking station that connects to a pair of wall speakers.

The Prophet's breath comes from the telephone and through the speakers as if he is sitting in the room with us. "Very well," he says. "I ask the young people to stand and stretch their legs before I start the lesson."

Immediately, all of the little kids jump to their feet. I'm still seething about Dirk as Amy stands on the other side of Mother. At least we're sitting behind him this time, so he doesn't bother her. The children twist side to side. Some reach for the ceiling.

"Better?" the Prophet asks as if he is there on the stage, even though I know he can't see us from his prison cell hundreds of miles away.

I check his portrait, just to make sure the eyes don't move.

The children nod, and Uncle Max walks past the Prophet's picture—the eyes remain still.

"We're ready to receive your word, Father," Dirk says as Uncle Max sits in a stuffed burgundy chair on the stage.

I shudder, annoyed all over again that Dirk touched me. As soon as I get home, I'm scrubbing my hand under the hottest water I can stand.

Amy reaches over Mother and pushes against my thigh to get my attention. She points to the back of the prayer room. I turn to look: Channing smiles and silently applauds. Tanner laughs to himself. Then I see Mother staring daggers at me and I quickly face forward, my face flushing hot.

"Be seated," the Prophet orders. "I'd ask that my people take a deep breath," the Prophet continues as the kids sit. On command, we all take a breath. As my lungs expand, I feel a little better. We exhale. "Another." We take another, and some of the anger seeps out of me. "Now smile." Everyone in the room forces a smile. Everyone. Mother gives me a look of warning, so I make myself smile, too. But it doesn't feel the same as when we all smiled without being ordered to do it.

"Today, we come to Third Nephi, Chapter Twelve," the Prophet says. Everyone's face relaxes as the sermon reverberates through the speakers. "This is where we are taught to always keep sweet."

I swallow hard. "Keep sweet" means we should act happy no matter how we really feel. We're supposed to hold in the sadness. When we keep sweet, we bottle up words of anger and never let them come spewing from our mouths. Meryl says I need a lot of work on that one.

"For if you keep sweet, you will conquer the evil inside," the Prophet continues.

I lower my head, guilty. I showed the evil inside when I stood up to Dirk. And the whole community saw it.

As the Prophet begins to read from the Book of Mormon, Tanner passes me an envelope.

My eyes question him. Is he *trying* to get me into trouble again?

He covers his lips with his index finger and then points for me to open it. While the Prophet explains in detail how the Beatitudes should "be our attitude," I slide the heavy cream card with raised gold lettering from the envelope.

It's an invitation. Goose bumps run up and down my arms. To Tanner and me. From the Santa Fe Music Festival. So many times, Tanner and I have talked about how someday we'd enter the competition for a chance to play in the festival. But we didn't enter. At least as far as I know, we didn't.

A smile stretches across my face. Mother sometimes records us so we can hear our mistakes. Did he use one of those? *How?* I mouth to Tanner. He shrugs with pride.

I skim the invitation again. We've been asked to play at the festival in five days. Five days. The best musicians in New Mexico. In five days.

"Happy birthday," Tanner whispers beneath the voice of the Prophet. He quickly looks forward.

"Gentry," Mother scolds softly, even though it wasn't me. Her tired eyes narrow. Seated down the row, Father grins slightly. His face is no longer red with anger. I wonder if he knows about the invitation. Mother clears her throat and points to the Prophet's portrait.

I quickly face forward.

"Make it right," the Prophet announces through the speakers.

I glance at the invitation. Another wave of excitement runs through me.

"Let go of your bad feelings."

My leg bobs with excitement. No bad feelings here. Father and Mother took some of us kids to the festival when we were little, and it's been our dream to play in it ever since.

"Be still," Mother hisses.

I sit on my hands and the invitation, trying to obey.

"Then the Lord will hear your prayers. You must keep sweet. So, smile. Smile."

"Smile," Uncle Max urges under his breath.

Everyone plasters a fake smile on again.

"For your smile is proof that you are chosen and blessed," the Prophet says. "Amen."

"Amen," we all repeat.

I inch to the edge of my seat, eager for the Prophet to dismiss us. I can't wait to talk to Tanner. Ask how he managed to enter us in the festival without me knowing about it. Discuss what we're going to play.

"I have received a holy revelation," the Prophet announces,

his voice somber. The Prophet talks with God and receives instructions directly from Him. We receive these revelations when he calls during our weekly prayer service or from Uncle Max, who visits the Prophet in prison monthly and speaks with him on the phone almost daily.

I lean against my seat, ready to hear the word of God.

The Prophet's breathing grows heavier through the speakers on the wall. "I have seen the evil of the outside world, and it is dark."

Mother's elbow knocks my side as she wraps her arms around herself.

"The outside world is jealous. They want to kill and destroy us."

My hand covers the invitation on my lap.

"None of you are safe from the evil influences of outsiders."

Uncle Max nods in agreement.

"Especially the women," the Prophet says.

Suddenly, it's as though the dull eyes of the Prophet's portrait are boring right through me. I can feel the letters on the festival invitation, brushing against my palm.

"I have seen your hearts, and you women are weak."

Men are strong. Women are weak. I've heard this ever since I can remember, even though I've beaten Kel at arm wrestling at least a dozen times. And he's the same age as me.

"Therefore, I declare, from this day forward, the women are too vulnerable to leave our community. From now on, you must stay inside our protective wall. It is so revealed."

The plastic chair presses into my shoulder blades as I bow my head. "Amen."

Tanner suddenly leans forward like the air's been knocked out of him. His face is as white as powdered milk.

"What's wrong?" I whisper, nudging him.

He looks like he's going to be sick. "You're a woman now," he moans.

I shake my head, not understanding.

"You." He points. "Woman."

And suddenly I understand. The Prophet's revelation. The festival. My birthday.

Tanner and I have dreamed about the festival for years. *Years.* And now we won't be able to go because I'm too old?

I want to scream, but then I remember the Prophet's warning about showing the evil inside. I glance over at Father's profile and take a deep breath. He's heard us go on about the festival so many times. He knows what it means to Tanner and me. I take another breath. If I can keep sweet, he'll have to let us go. If I follow the spirit of the Prophet, everything will be fine.

3.

The mothers are making a spaghetti dinner for my birthday—
one of my favorites. But I won't get a single bite. Father had
punished me before I could get two words out. *Nothing to eat
until you learn how to keep sweet, young lady.* He wouldn't even
give me a chance to explain. He didn't want to hear my "excuses."
He cut me off before I could bring up the festival. Thanks a lot,
Dirk the Jerk.

My mouth waters from the smell of Mother Lenora's fresh-
baked bread. Six loaves of white. Six loaves of wheat. All in a
line across our kitchen countertop.

The room is clear of kids, except for the girls helping with
dinner. I stand at the sink, rinsing bowls under the faucet,
while Meryl dumps large cans of spinach into a heavy pot. She
turns her head away from the stove as she stirs and covers her
nose as the bitter smell fills the kitchen. I'm so hungry that
even the spinach smells good to me.

Seconds tick by on the clock over the sink. The emptiness in my stomach makes the waiting worse.

From the family room, Amy squeals, "Yes!" to the little ones. She's been playing the memory game—testing their recall of the names of our many relatives—with old family photos.

The Prophet warns that idle hands are the devil's workshop, so I finish washing the mixing bowls and set them on the drying rack. I check the clock again.

"You won't make time go any faster," Mother says, lifting Baby Bill from the bassinet she keeps in the kitchen.

"What's taking them so long?" I ask. Father owns a construction company and checks his work sites with Tanner every Sunday after lunch. With so many mouths to feed, Father made Tanner and most of my other brothers quit school when they were around my age so they could help out. They've been gone so long this afternoon, I'm hoping that means Tanner's been talking to Father about the festival.

I rock from side to side, unable to contain my excitement at the thought of actually playing in the Santa Fe Music Festival. How many years have Tanner and I talked about that moment?

"Just keep the spirit of the Prophet, and you'll find your patience," Mother says. Then her voice cracks. "All those years in that horrible cell." My swaying stops. The Prophet has been in prison for almost eleven years now. I barely remember what it was like with the Prophet living among us, but Mother acts like the outsiders took him away yesterday. She clutches Baby Bill tight to her chest. "The Prophet never asks what's taking so long." Mother's looking at me now with exhausted eyes. The wave of golden hair above her forehead has gone flat in the hot kitchen.

The Prophet teaches we should all strive to achieve the heavenly virtue of patience—one more thing Meryl says I stink at. She's looking at me, too.

"I'm sorry, Mother." I sigh. "I'll try to be more patient."

"They're home," someone yells.

"See?" Mother says with a smile, like she's proven her point.

Meryl returns to her stirring, while the other mothers jump to action.

Without a word, Father stomps into the kitchen to wash his hands at the sink. Tanner trails him and zips by me without making eye contact. He retreats down the stairs to the basement so he can wash his hands, too.

My shoulders sink.

"Dinnertime," Mother Lenora announces through the house intercom. We used to just shout this, but Father couldn't stand all the yelling.

After he dries his hands on a kitchen towel, Father is the first to receive a plate. Father's always first. My other brothers and sisters line up behind him.

Some of the younger kids are crying from hunger pangs. I'd like to tell them I know how they feel, but I'm too busy with the older girls, filling cups with ice water and placing giant tubs of butter on the long, long tables. We have two rectangular tables right next to the kitchen. They sit side by side, both lined with hungry kids ranging in age from one to nineteen. After we get plates for the younger ones, the older ones have to help them eat.

Mother Dee, Father's third wife, stands next to the cooktop. She props a plate on the curve of her pregnant belly and gives Father a heaping scoop of spinach. Next to the pile of limp green leaves, she mounds a swirl of pasta on the plate. My stomach growls as Mother Dee sprinkles Parmesan cheese on Father's spaghetti. She gives the cheese an extra shake. Then, another. Some of the kids grumble since the cheese will probably run out by the time the last ones are served. No cheese means plain pasta and zero flavor.

But Father always gets the most food, and if he wants more, he says he can have it. He's already proven his worthiness to the Prophet and holds the priesthood. He has a say in whether every single one of us gets to go to heaven or has to spend an eternity burning in hell. Personally, I think he should get all the Parmesan cheese he wants.

I'm quickly moving down the long tables, handing out the

paper napkins someone else forgot. As I finish, Father tucks a loose hair behind Mother Dee's ear. She smiles up at him. My mother, who's feeding Baby Bill, turns away.

Near the end of the line, I spot Tanner stick his finger into his mouth and pretend to gag. He does that sometimes when Father shows Mother Dee affection. She's only a few years older than Tanner and has the darkest hair of my father's wives, plus the greenest eyes I've ever seen. My brother won't admit it, but I think he had a crush on her before she became our mother.

As the line continues to wind behind him, Father takes his place at the head of the table. He doesn't wait for anyone. He starts eating.

At the other table, Amy makes faces at the little kids, while they await their food. She sticks out her tongue and pulls tightly on her eyes behind her glasses. A few giggles erupt. I can't help but laugh.

"Gentry," Father mumbles through his chewing. "Have a seat."

I wipe my hand on my skirt. "Yes, Father," I say and pass off the napkins to one of my half sisters. My heart races as I march around the table and head toward him. It's an honor to be asked to sit beside Father. Too bad I don't get to eat, too.

Mother Lenora, who is sitting next to Father, lets out an exasperated sigh when I take the seat across from her. Father takes a slice of bread from the basket, and my mouth waters again. I dig my fingernails into my hands to keep from snatching a piece and gobbling it up.

But I don't have to struggle for long. Mother Lenora passes the bread to her son Kel. My half brother takes a slice and then passes it on to his twin, Kate. It goes farther and farther down the table. Away from me.

I remind myself to keep sweet and force a smile even though it's hard with everyone eating in front of me.

"Hannah," Father says as my mother sits next to me. "Give that plate to your daughter and get yourself another."

My stomach growls eagerly as Mother sets her plate before me. I snatch the napkin and place it across my lap. "Thank you, Father." I don't want to give him a chance to change his mind. I pick up my fork.

Mother Lenora jabs her finger in my direction. "She's being punished."

Father swallows his food. "Her punishment is over. I trust she's learned her lesson," he says and eyes me.

I quickly nod.

"I'll get another plate," Mother says, and I can hear the smile in her voice.

I want to hug Father, but we're not supposed to. So I take a bite instead, savoring the salty cheese and pasta on my tongue.

Father laughs. "Is it that good?"

"Yes, sir," I say through a mouthful of pasta.

Mother Lenora shakes her head and shoves another forkful into her round face. I want to ask Father about the festival, but I don't want to get my plate taken away before I have a chance to finish dinner. I decide to eat first.

When my mother returns with a new plate and much smaller portions, a part of me feels guilty that I took hers. "I had lunch. You didn't," she says, as if reading my mind in that eerie way mothers sometimes do.

Mother Dee blots her forehead when everyone has a plate and takes her seat next to Mother Lenora. Mother Dee's portion sizes are almost as large as Father's.

Mother nudges me under the table to keep me from staring.

I take my last bite of pasta when Father does and watch him gulp his ice water. With so many other kids around, I may not get another chance to talk to him about the festival. "Father."

He sets his glass on the table. "If you're going to ask me about the festival, your brother already did."

"And?" I ask hopefully.

"And it's out of my hands." He wipes his mouth with his napkin. "I talked to Uncle Max, and he said no."

The hope drains from me as quickly as it came. "Did you tell him how important this is to us?"

Father nods. "And he says, with you being a woman now, it's in direct violation of the Prophet's revelation."

It feels like a solid lump has formed in my stomach. I shouldn't have eaten so fast. "But the festival's only a few days away."

"You'd defy the Prophet?" Mother Lenora asks as she mops up spinach juice with her bread.

I shake my head. "It's not like that."

"How is it then?" she asks, her voice laced with accusation.

Mother Dee places a hand on her belly. "I've heard it's gotten so much worse. The outsiders are now kidnapping and torturing people like us."

All of my life, the Prophet has told us the outsiders are evil. They're jealous we're God's chosen and want to hurt us. I've only been outside our walls a few times, including the one time to the festival, but that was a while ago and with a large group.

I hate to admit it: I *am* a little scared to go. But this has been our dream for years, and I probably won't get a chance to do anything like this ever again. "Tanner will be there. He'll look out for me, I know it."

"You would defy the Prophet then," Mother Lenora says, her voice tightening.

Mother Dee swirls pasta onto her fork. "The outsiders have trained their dogs to attack us. Did you know that?"

36

"And she'd go out there willingly," Mother Lenora says, mocking me. "Wouldn't you?"

As I push the spinach from side to side on my plate, I can feel Mother Dee and Mother Lenora glaring at me, ready to pounce if—*when*—I say the wrong thing. I look to Father, but he's buttering another piece of bread.

What can I say to get them to stop looking at me? What's the right response? I finally settle on, "What's the question again?"

Mother Lenora clucks her tongue. "Honestly, Hannah. If my daughter talked with such disrespect, I'd rip her from this table and beat some sense into her."

I drop my fork. It rattles against the plate. As one of my mothers, Mother Lenora has every right to discipline me. And she hits so hard, it makes you wish you were never born. My hand wads the napkin on my lap.

Mother sets her fork down gently. "Thank you for your opinion, Lenora. But she knows perfect obedience produces perfect faith. Gentry's a little excited, that's all."

"I was excited, too," Father admits, channeling everyone's attention back to him.

"You were?" I ask, surprised.

He nods and swallows the rest of his bread. Mother Lenora's lips tighten. She won't get to lay a hand on me now. Not over this. My fingers unclench the napkin.

Mother Dee resumes her chewing as Father continues, "When Tanner asked if he could surprise you and enter a recording of the two of you into the competition, I said yes. But I did not know then that the Prophet would make this pronouncement." Father takes another drink of water. "This family will obey the Prophet's revelation. You're staying home. That's final."

"But, Father—"

"No buts." Father's green eyes bore straight into mine. "The devil is tempting you, Gentry. I expect you will make the right choice and follow God's word."

I lower my head. "Yes, Father."

Mother pats my hand. "Just put it on a shelf and pray about it."

I roll my eyes. That's our community's response to anything difficult. But I don't want to put this on a shelf.

"Gentry will keep sweet," Father says, confident, even though I'm not. "Especially once she sees her birthday present."

My head lifts. "Wait. What?"

He smiles. "You didn't think I forgot, did you?"

Actually, yes, I did. "No, of course not," I say.

"If you're finished, come with me," he says. "Hannah will clear your plate."

Mother Lenora turns to Mother Dee. "Do you know anything about this?" Mother Dee shakes her head.

I search the table for Tanner. If there's a secret in our family, he's usually the first to know about it. I find him over at the other table, holding Baby Bill while he eats. *You're gonna love it,* he mouths.

Mother interrupts, "Your father's waiting." With a soft smile, she nods for me to follow him into the living room.

I slip between the tables, past my talking and punching and laughing brothers and sisters before stepping down into our sunken living area that's off the kitchen. After dinner, my entire family will gather here in front of the large portrait of the Prophet for Sunday night devotional.

Father reaches behind his La-Z-Boy as I round the mismatched sofas where my mothers sit. He pulls out a large rectangular case.

My heart beats fast.

"Hey, what is it?" Amy asks, stumbling into the room behind us.

"I don't know yet," I say, though I suspect I do. A grin tugs at the corners of my mouth.

"Hurry," she says, breathless. "Open it."

I look to Father as he sets it on the floor. "It won't open itself," he says.

My fingers reach for the small zippers as I crouch, and I slowly slide them outward. A small silver latch hides beneath the zippers. I look up at Father with anticipation.

"Go on," he encourages. I slide the latch to the right and open the case. Resting in the blue velvet lining is a honey-colored, full-size violin.

I blink a few times to make sure I'm not dreaming. My hand covers my mouth. "Oh, Father," I say through my fingers.

Amy gasps.

Father's smiling. "I bought it at the violin shop in Albuquerque. Tanner helped pick it out."

"Oh, Father," I say again, lifting the instrument from the case. I pluck the A string. The sound is so rich, I nearly cry. "It's perfect. Thank you."

"Told you she'd like it," Tanner says. "It's Hungarian. The shopkeeper said it's over a hundred years old."

"You're kidding," I say, even though I know music's the one thing we don't kid about.

Everyone starts coming in for prayer time. "What is it?" some of my siblings ask as they barge into the room. "What did she get?"

I proudly hold up my new instrument for them to see.

"You spoil her, Conway," Mother Lenora grumbles. "What use is that?"

I'm so happy; her words can't keep me from grinning.

Father stands tall. "Uncle Max was very impressed with Tanner and Gentry during today's service."

"He was?" I ask, shocked again. Nothing impresses the Vulture, except himself. And, of course, the Prophet.

Father winks at me.

Mother Dee elbows Mother Lenora's broad side. "I received a sewing machine on my thirteenth birthday."

Mother Lenora nods. "And I received a quilt and baby blankets. Those are appropriate gifts for a future wife and mother." Mother Lenora plops on the floral sofa, making it sag on one side. "Not a violin."

They're right: Girls usually receive something for their future home. According to the Prophet, the highest honor a girl can hope for is to get married. And then, having babies. I glance at the spit-up stain down the front of Mother Lenora's dress. That's all I'm supposed to live for and dream about: marriage and babies. I know it's wrong, but I sometimes wonder if that's enough for me.

"I think it's a lovely gift," my mother says as she enters the room and takes her place on the navy-blue sofa. Her upright piano sits against the wall behind her.

Mother Lenora huffs. "That's because you're the one who introduced the devilry of music to your children in the first place." I hate that she's trying to pick this old fight. Again. Mother was raised in a more progressive home than my other mothers, and they won't *ever* let her forget it. Music was not only allowed when Mother was growing up, but also encouraged.

Mother's hands curl against the sofa, but she nods. As the second wife, my mother must respect Mother Lenora's position as the first wife, no matter how absurd or unfair.

Most of my siblings are on the floor now, shoving for space on the carpet.

Meryl is behind Mother, holding the hands of two of our younger half sisters. She stops when she sees. "It's so very beautiful, Father."

That returns the smile to Mother's face.

Father turns to me. "I'm sorry we couldn't afford to buy you a new bow. Your old one will do?"

"Of course," I say. "Thank you, Father."

"Play something, will you?" He gestures to my new violin. My *new* violin. Despite what my other mothers say, it's the perfect gift.

Father nods. "Tanner, you too."

My brother slides one of the toddlers off his lap and jumps from the floor. "Yes, sir."

I pull the bow from my old case and slide my instrument under my chin for the first time. It fits like it was made for me. The smooth neck rests perfectly in the curve between my index finger and thumb. Like I hoped it would.

Tanner lifts his instrument. "Would you care for a hymn, Father?"

"Musicians' choice," Father replies as he sits in his chair and rocks back and forth.

"'Jerusalem's Ridge'?" Tanner suggests and turns to me. "You take the melody. Let's see what you can do with that thing."

I smile at Tanner's challenge.

With a deep breath, we count off and start with ten staccato strokes of the bow. Then, I fly. At least, it feels like flying to me. I soar straight out of the box I'm expected to stay in when I'm not playing my music.

My fingers run across the fingerboard with the old bluegrass tune. The timbre of my new violin is so intense, I hardly notice my family clapping to the rhythm of our song. I glance at Amy. She's dancing with the little ones, while Kel and Kate march in place. Tanner and I keep pace, weaving notes between us without slowing until we reach the last few measures and end with a harmonious chord.

Almost everyone is clapping and on their feet. Father whistles so loud, the little kids cover their ears. Even Meryl is grinning and cheering. I'm so happy, it doesn't even bother me that Mother Lenora and Mother Dee are frowning at us. The flying feeling refuses to leave me.

Under the applause and shouts of encouragement, Tanner leans in with a whisper, "You know there's no way we're staying home now."

He comes away, grinning from ear to ear, and takes a bow. Is he saying what I think he's saying?

"Gentry, bow," Amy commands. I do as I'm told. My brothers and sisters go wild with cheers. My chest swells.

I cradle my precious new violin against my body and wonder if it could even be possible. Sneaking out is dangerous. And there's the God Squad with their giant pickup trucks and guns. Way too dangerous.

But we've been dreaming of the festival for years, and now I have the perfect violin. We may not get another chance.

Tanner's right. We *have* to go.

4.

I sit next to Meryl on the steps of Watchful Academy, our community's school, and nervously flip through the pages of my textbook as we patiently wait for Uncle Max to signal the start of morning lessons. It's the day of the festival, and somehow, Tanner plans to sneak me out of our community. He gave me a wink in the kitchen, his little promise, before the sun lit the sky.

But now, the sun's rays already shine strong behind the Sangre de Cristo Mountains. My heart flip-flops in anticipation of Tanner's arrival. The younger kids play tag and slip-slide across the gravel parking lot in front of the school. The older boys, who aren't off at the construction sites, goof off under the shade of the junipers. Separated by the length of the parking lot, the older girls stand and giggle beneath another set of trees, sometimes stealing glances at the boys.

My fingers poke through the holes where our teachers have cut sections from the book to protect us from the outsiders' lies. Meryl points to the fading outline of the moon against the blue sky and furrows her brow. She leans in with a whisper, "Did you know the outsiders tell their kids that a man walked on the moon?"

"You're kidding," I say with a laugh.

Meryl shakes her head.

I don't know where she gets this stuff. "And they actually *believe* it?"

My sister shrugs. "I know. Weird, huh?"

The bell rings, and Meryl jumps to her feet. I slap my textbook shut and scoop my other books from the porch before standing. Where's Tanner? We're supposed to play at the festival this morning. He should be here by now.

But I don't see his truck. I look right and then left, only to see a blue tarp, flapping in the breeze. There's lots of these tarps in Watchful since families are constantly growing, and there's always a need for more space. Since the men can only get help from the rest of the community on Work Saturdays, the construction projects never seem to end.

The nearest tarp is partially tacked to the unfinished addition on Channing Snell's house. A few days ago, he and his family moved in the middle of the night without saying a word to anyone.

I clench my hands. I can't believe Channing didn't tell us where he was going or, at least, say good-bye.

Uncle Max steps outside and flaps toward the little kids. "Young people, inside," he orders.

Their feet pound up the stairs before they rush past us and run inside the school.

"The young men will have survival class today," Uncle Max announces. The boys quiet instantly and line up in two rows along the gravel. I search for my half brother Kel. After the last survival class, he locked himself in the bathroom for two hours. He wouldn't say why. His face is pale now.

Suddenly, a scarred hand touches my shoulder. His hot breath smells like rotten onions. Dirk. Where did he come from?

He gives me a slimy smile and squeezes my shoulder, making my stomach turn. I glance at Uncle Max, but he's not looking at me. Nobody's looking at me. Dirk should know he's not supposed to touch me. We all know. From the time we're little, girls are taught that boys are snakes—never to be touched. Why won't he leave me alone?

He releases me and clomps down the stairs toward the waiting boys.

"The young ladies will meet for home economics," Uncle Max says, and then descends the stairs to give instructions to the Jerk.

My jaw clenches. I hate him. I hate him. I *hate* him.

Meryl nudges me toward the front door. "Let's go."

"Did you see what Dirk did?" I ask under my breath.

Meryl shakes her head. "I have no idea what you're talking about."

"I have to tell Uncle Max."

She sighs. "Don't be so dramatic, Gentry."

My mouth goes dry.

"I'm sure you're just making something out of nothing," she says and hurries me inside the main hallway.

Was I? I clutch my books against my chest and wipe my free hand against my skirt, letting my sister lead me inside Watchful Academy. It didn't *feel* like nothing.

The sterile smell surrounds us. A few years after he was arrested, the Prophet instructed Uncle Max to pull all the children from public school and convert the Prophet's home into our school. Even though I've never known anything else, it still looks like a house to me.

Meryl and I walk quietly with the other girls past the kitchen and make a left into what used to be the Prophet's living room.

By the time I sit at my desk in the third row, I wonder if I really was making something out of nothing. But then, I remember his hot, stinky breath against my cheek and shudder.

Mrs. Whittier stands watch at the front of the classroom as

the rest of my classmates enter. Her spindly fingers touch the hair above her ear, right where it's starting to gray. She's the first of the Vulture's twelve wives. "Ladies, put your textbooks beneath your chairs and pull out your notebooks. You will need paper and a pen to take notes on the lesson."

Meryl quickly retrieves her blank paper and a pen, while the other girls grumble around me.

Mrs. Whittier sucks in her cheeks. "Ladies," she scolds, pacing in front of the large portrait of the Prophet, like the one that hangs in the prayer room and in every home and at the front of every classroom. "You should feel honored the Prophet has taken the time to record these instructions for us from his prison cell. My husband had to travel many days to get these important lessons."

She stops pacing. Her head moves side to side on a neck that's almost as long as the Vulture's. "He spent many hours with the Prophet to receive these revelations, and you will take thorough notes. Your summary paper is due tomorrow's class."

More groans. Everyone knows the messages from the Prophet are boring. He drones in this low, expressionless voice that puts everyone to sleep. "I hate this," my half sister Kate whines under her breath.

"Enough!" Mrs. Whittier yells. Kate's eyes go wide as Mrs. Whittier rushes toward her, ruler in hand, and swats her arm

49

with a *smack*. Kate cries out. We all jump. Mrs. Whittier strikes her again, this time on her hand, leaving a straight, red welt along the top. "Another outburst and it's the strap for all of you."

I cover my mouth to hide the sound of my breath. No one dares say a word. Kate quietly wipes the tears from her cheeks and pulls paper and a pencil from her desk.

When she's satisfied everyone is quiet, Mrs. Whittier stalks to the front of the classroom and sits in her chair. She lowers her ruler and presses play on the cassette player. The tape rolls for a second and then there's a popping sound as the Prophet begins:

> *"These words have been given to me by God. I am merely the messenger of His word. May He be the teacher of this home economics class."*

"Amen," Mrs. Whittier says, now solemn.

I glance at the portrait of the Prophet in his dark suit and swallow hard.

"Amen," we repeat.

> *"Dear sisters, marriage is God's will, spoken through the Prophet. He will match each one of you with a priesthood*

man. You will help build Zion by bringing forth children in

your marriage."

Kate takes frantic notes with her welted hand even though it's not necessary. We all know a girl's primary purpose in this life is to get married to a priesthood man and have as many children as possible in preparation for the next life.

"You belong to the Prophet and only he can hear the call of

the Lord and place you where you belong."

Girls around me nod. I shift uncomfortably. The Prophet chooses who we marry and when. I start doodling on my page and check the clock. Where is Tanner?

"Your husband will rule over you, as the Prophet rules over

all. You must keep sweet and not weigh down your husband

with your troubles. For knowing that you are pleasing your

priesthood head will bring you the ultimate happiness."

I look at my page—at my doodles—and realize I've drawn a hangman.

"But a man may only have a wife if he holds the priesthood.

If he becomes an apostate and loses the priesthood, so also

shall he lose his wives and children."

Meryl nudges me with a whisper, "I heard that's what happened to Channing Snell's family."

"What?" I ask under my breath. That's not what I heard.

My sister sighs. "You know. About your age. Dark hair. Freckle face."

I nod. "I *know* who he is." Before Channing started hanging out with Tanner so much, we used to fish together in the creek on the other side of the hill. But that came to an end when the Prophet had a revelation that the devil controlled the water when it was used for pleasure. Mother made me stop fishing with Channing after that.

Meryl cups her hand around her mouth and leans in. "Uncle Max and the Prophet declared his father an apostate and kicked him out."

My breath lurches. That's impossible. Mr. Snell has five wives and almost forty children. The Snells are one of Watchful's most righteous families.

Meryl thumps her index finger against the desk. "That's why Channing and his mothers and his brothers and sisters all went into hiding. So their father can't find them and kidnap them."

I shake my head. "Mother said the Prophet sent them to the mountains to pray for us."

"Why would the Prophet do that?" Meryl gives me a condescending look and shrugs. "Believe what you want."

If Mr. Snell really is an apostate now, he can never return to our community again. I bite my lip. Poor Channing.

"Is there something you'd like to share with the rest of the class, ladies?" Mrs. Whittier has paused the tape. Her eyes narrow, wrinkling her face as she glares at us.

She snatches her ruler as she stands. Kate shrinks to my left. My heart thuds against my ribs.

Mrs. Whittier starts toward me. I hide my hands under the desk.

"Sorry to interrupt," Tanner says, breaking her steps. Mrs. Whittier's head turns on her long neck until she sees my brother. He leans in the doorway. Finally.

The ruler lowers at her side. I can breathe.

"Is there something you need, Mr. Forrester?" Even though Mrs. Whittier is over twenty years older than Tanner, she must treat him with respect. Ever since my brother turned fourteen—when most boys receive the Aaronic priesthood—his opinion has been seen as more valuable than any woman's, even Mother's.

"Gentry is needed at home," he says.

I bite down a smile. So, this is how Tanner's going to get me out of here?

Mrs. Whittier returns to her desk. "I do hope everything is all right?"

My brother nods without betraying any information. "Thank you."

I can see Mrs. Whittier's lips twist, as if she's forcing herself not to be disrespectful and ask for more.

"Then, I'll go, too," Meryl adds, placing her notebook inside her desk.

I shake my head. "I'm sure it's fine."

"If there's something wrong, I want to help," Meryl says.

My eyes dart to Tanner.

"It's Amy," he says firmly, and Meryl stops moving.

She looks at me with hurt in her eyes. When Amy was little, she wanted to go to school, but Uncle Max wouldn't let her. She would throw these huge fits. Sometimes, they'd get so bad, Mother would pull me out of school. As much as my other brothers and sisters tried, it seemed only I could calm her.

Meryl pulls her paper out again with a sigh. "On second thought, I think I'd like to stay and hear the rest of the lesson."

"Don't just sit there," Mrs. Whittier barks. "Leave your books. Your sister will bring them home."

"Yes, ma'am," Meryl and I say in unison. I bury my paper inside my desk and join Tanner at the door.

As my brother and I hurry along the main hallway in silence, I can hear the voice of the Prophet resume and echo:

"You ladies belong to the Prophet . . ."

The doors creak as we exit Watchful Academy. When I know we're alone, I finally breathe. Tanner's truck is the only car in the parking lot.

"You're late," I say.

My brother's boots crunch the gravel as he steps to his rear bumper. He glances around to make sure no one's looking and pops the cover on the bed of his pickup truck. "Get in."

In the back of Tanner's truck, there's a couple of cement sacks and a stack of quilts next to a canister of gasoline. I shiver. "What? No way."

Tanner rolls his eyes and lowers his voice. "You didn't think I'd get you past the God Squad with you riding in the front seat, did you?"

The thought of lying beneath the metal cover—trapped in the hot darkness—makes my heart clench. I shake my head hard. "Forget it."

"It's just to get you past the wall, silly. I'll let you out when I know we're in the clear."

I wipe my hands across my skirt and peer at the truck bed again. I can feel the darkness crushing me already.

"Come on," Tanner says, pushing me toward the truck. "We're late."

My hands ball into fists as I try to plant my feet on the slipping gravel. "And that's *my* fault?" I ask, my voice rising.

"Is there a problem here?" a voice caws. Tanner and I both go still. The Vulture looks down on us from the Watchful Academy porch.

Tanner shifts away from me. "Uh, no, Uncle Max." He clears his throat. "Gentry and I were just having a little argument. Everything's fine now. We were just leaving," he says and rounds the pickup.

"Not so fast," Uncle Max says as he descends the porch steps and edges closer.

I lower my eyes to my dusty shoes. I can feel the Vulture's stare—like I'm his next roadkill feast.

"Aren't you supposed to be in class, young lady?"

"I've come to fetch her," Tanner says. "To help with Amy."

"Is that right?" the Vulture murmurs.

I can tell he wants me to say something. My eyes go as high

as his bumpy neck, but I can't meet his gaze. I know he'll see right through me. "Yes, sir."

His Adam's apple bobs up and down. "Must be difficult to be the one called upon to deal with the family imbecile."

My neck stiffens as I meet his hardened eyes. "She's not—"

Tanner bumps me from behind, stopping me with a false laugh. "You were right all along. Amy's blanket *was* in the back of the truck."

"What?" I ask, turning to him.

Tanner holds up one of the colorful quilts, his eyes willing me to catch on to his lie.

I smirk and nod. "Told you."

"Yes," he says, nodding to Uncle Max. "And now I'll never hear the end of it. If you'll excuse us?"

The Vulture says nothing for a second and then gestures to the truck with his spindly arms.

My brother closes the cover on the bed of his truck as I hop into the front seat, relieved not to be locked in the back.

"Way to go." Tanner jumps in and tosses the blanket at me. "Now he's watching us."

The engine turns and roars.

"What are we going to do?" I ask as Tanner spins the truck away from the school.

"What do you think? We're gonna have to drive by the house, so we don't raise any suspicion."

I check the truck's clock. "But we're already running late."

"Yeah, well, you should've thought about that *before* you threw a fit." As he drives, he nods at the blanket in my hands. "Crawl into the back. Lie on the floorboard and cover up."

"What? Why?" I ask, dropping the quilt as we're nearing our house.

"Hurry." He shoves the blanket toward me again. "We still have to get past Buckley."

My heart beats fast as I think of Buckley's harsh, red face— his black God Squad uniform—and the gun he keeps strapped to his hip. I scramble to the back and squish my body between the front and back seats, landing on the floor. I quickly throw the quilt over my head, encasing me in the smell of Mother's detergent and Tanner's gasoline.

I make sure my feet are hidden beneath the blanket's wedding-ring pattern and lay my ear to the floorboard. Rocks clink against the undercarriage of the truck as Tanner bumps across the dirt roads.

I can feel the truck slow. "We're at the gate," Tanner says. "Pray they just wave us through."

We stop. The window rolls down. My heart thrums inside my ears.

"Tanner," Buckley says from outside. "Where you headed today?" His voice moves like he's looking inside the truck. I hold my breath, willing myself not to move.

"Chimayó," Tanner answers. "Helping out on that remodel."

Sweat runs down my back, and I pray Buckley and his God Squad don't discover my hiding place. I keep praying, praying and holding my breath until I almost black out.

All of a sudden, someone taps the side of the truck. "Move along," Buckley orders.

I manage a small breath as I hear the window seal shut.

We bump in the ruts of the road.

After a few minutes, maybe ten, the blanket comes off my face. I gasp as the light streams in through the windows and blinds me. I'm quick to check; it's only Tanner. The truck is still moving, but the road now feels smooth beneath us. My brother faces forward, but I can see his mischievous smile.

From my knees, I peek over the seat and see the numbers on the clock: 9:22. We're supposed to play at ten o'clock sharp. It will take us at least forty minutes to get out of the hills. "We'll never make it," I say as the red, scrub-covered hills zip by our windows. I look back, but Watchful is already out of sight.

Tanner doesn't seem fazed. Instead, his eyes are wide with awe, taking in the world around us. He pats the front seat. "Come up, kid," he says. "Come see the world with me."

5.

It's been over an hour since we left Watchful, and Tanner's no longer in awe. He's lost, which means *we're* lost. And late.

We've been driving the narrow streets of Santa Fe but are nowhere closer to the Plaza. We pass the Collected Works Bookstore for the third time, and Tanner turns right again. I point at the bookstore. "Haven't we passed this already?"

"No," Tanner says, stopping for pedestrians in the crosswalk. "I don't know." He slaps his steering wheel in frustration. "Where did all these people come from?"

The sidewalks are full of smiling people in shorts and sleeveless tops. I touch the upper part of my arm, making sure it's still covered by the sleeve of my dress. These are the outsiders the Prophet says are going to try to destroy us at the end of the world.

Clusters of them pass—left and right—in front of our truck.

Every one of them knows where they're going. My fingers drop and dig into the seat.

"Move already." Tanner sighs loudly. "Come *on*."

A girl a little older than me crosses the street in jean shorts, her tanned legs bare to the world. Her hair has been cut short. But that's not what shocks me most. "Her shirt," I whisper, seeing her in red. Not long ago, the Prophet proclaimed the color red was reserved for Jesus Christ. We may never wear it. Ever. My eyes follow the girl as she enters a café. I look down at my ankle-length, mint-green dress and tug on my skirt. "Maybe we should just go home."

"Finally," Tanner says, ignoring me, and gases the truck.

We go a couple of blocks and Tanner makes a quick turn. "We need help," he says and screeches into a nearby parking lot, where a massive tan-stoned building shadows us. Tanner cuts the engine.

I look upward to the spires, touching the blue sky, and shift. "What are we doing here?"

Tanner jumps from the truck. "Asking for directions."

Someone walks past my window, and I startle. "You're going to *talk* to them?"

"It's that or keep driving in circles." He gives me a little smile and gestures toward the huge stone building. "It's a church. How bad can it be?"

He slams his door, and I jump again. My brother pops open the hatch on the back of his truck, and in the side mirror, I can see he's retrieved our violin cases.

He opens my door.

I shake my head. "I'll wait here."

"We're already late. It doesn't make any sense for me to come back for you."

I eye him, wary.

"I'll do the talking," he says and hands over my violin case. "You want to play, right?"

In spite of my head telling me no, I nod and slip from the truck. I trail my brother along the winding path, edged with tiny yellow flowers. We pass a group of outsiders sitting on benches; my shoulders tighten as I hurry to match Tanner's pace. We walk by a stone marker that says LORETTO, before approaching a pair of carved wooden doors. I grip the handle on my violin case tight and follow him inside the air-conditioned chapel.

People are milling around the elongated room, taking pictures and whispering. Some of them glance at me a little longer than necessary and then avert their eyes. But I'm more concerned about the missing picture of the Prophet. Where is he?

Tanner nudges me toward the back pew. "Stay here," he says, and charges toward a person wearing a gold name tag on the far side of the chapel. A group of people surrounds the man as he talks about one of the paintings.

I sit on the bench and lay my case across my lap, hugging it to my stomach. My eyes dart around, trying to take in all the details from the front to the back of the room: the elaborate white marble carving and gold cross; the candles flickering in rows; people kneeling before them in prayer; the colorful stained-glass windows; a carving of a bearded man in a white robe. On both sides of the chapel, there's also a progression of small carvings that tell the story of Jesus's fateful journey to the cross. I shift in the pew. There's not a single picture or carving of the Prophet.

"Are you familiar with our Miraculous Staircase?" a woman asks. My heart beats fast. She hovers in the aisle, wearing all black from head to toe with a cross around her neck. She's even more covered than I am, but nobody seems to stare at her. She doesn't move.

I scoot down the pew, away from her, and shake my head.

She smiles softly, creasing the lines around her mouth. "When the chapel was completed in the late 1800s, there was no way for the choir to get to the second floor. For nine days, the sisters prayed morning, noon, and night. Then, on the final day, a strange man appeared." She points to the narrow spiral staircase with two full turns and made entirely from wood. "He built this without nails. There's no means of support, and yet it stands firm. When he finished, he disappeared forever."

From my seat, I can see the lighter underbelly of the twisting, turning staircase. "Who was it?" I ask, my quiet voice echoing.

She presses her hands together. "No one knows for sure, but many believe God sent the stranger in response to our prayers." She smiles again.

I smile with the realization. "It was the Prophet," I answer. I'm sure of it. Everyone everywhere knows he does the work of God on earth.

The woman shakes her head. "I'm sorry?"

"The Prophet," I say again. "You know? It's not the same one we have now, since it was so long ago." My hands tap the top of my violin case. "Our Prophet's in prison."

The woman's eyes widen.

I shake my head. "It's really not his fault. It's the outsiders. They—"

"Gentry," my brother scolds, eyeing the woman and then me. "We have to go."

I grasp the handle of my violin case and rise. The woman clears the aisle and then her throat. "Peace be with you, then."

"Thank you," I say, and my brother leads me by the arm outside the doors into the shadow of the chapel.

He stops abruptly. Bees buzz in the tiny yellow flowers near our legs. He releases me with a huff and pinches his fingers together. "We've been this close all along." He swings his violin case to the other hand and shakes his head, his face falling. "We're so late."

We've worked so hard. We've come all this way. "What are you saying?"

He gives me a sly smile. "I'm saying we better run," he says and takes off before I can react.

"Tanner," I shout after him, but he's already to the street corner. I start after him. "Tanner, wait," I yell, my case bobbing at my side, intermittently smacking against my leg.

My brother runs up the Santa Fe Trail, zipping in and out of people. I try to catch up, but he's too fast. I rush past outdoor vendors selling wood carvings and colorful blankets. Tanner turns left and disappears behind the adobe buildings.

When I finally reach the corner and turn, I almost bump right into him. "Found it," he says, proud.

I wipe the sweat from the back of my neck. People are everywhere. I mean everywhere. I don't think I've ever seen so many outsiders all in one place.

They mill and sit in the center of the Plaza with its grass and trees surrounded by adobe shops and restaurants. Classical music pipes through the outdoor speakers. "Let's find the stage," Tanner suggests, and we cross the street with the crowd. My pulse runs as I sense the awkward sideways glances of strangers. I can't hear their whispers beneath the music and laughter.

We reach the edge of the Plaza, where there's even more people. Nearby, a mother stands on the grass, blowing iridescent bubbles from a tiny wand. A toddler stumbles as he tries to catch the bubbles before they float away on the light breeze. The smell of hot grease from an Indian fry bread stand fills the air. A vendor pours strings of honey across a pillow of blue corn and hands the grease-stained plate to a little boy. My mouth waters with hunger.

"There," Tanner says, pointing to the covered stage on the other side of the square. The string quartet we hear through the speakers is playing there now. We weave our way through the crowd, past a stone obelisk that marks the center of the Plaza. On this side of the marker, most everybody sits on blankets or lawn chairs, listening to the musicians play.

I swallow hard as we edge around to the back of the stage. The registration table is several feet behind it. A woman in a wide-brimmed hat sits behind the table with a girl, who looks about my age. The girl has black hair and wears a sundress that shows off her dark skin. I clutch my violin case to my chest.

"Uh, hi," Tanner says as we approach the table.

The woman smiles wide. "Here for the festival, I presume?" she asks, pointing to our violin cases.

"Yes," Tanner says, placing his case on the ground. "But we're really late. I got lost and—"

"Oh, you must be the Forresters," she says, flipping through a list of names.

"Yes. Yes, ma'am."

The woman thunks the end of her pencil against the list. "I'm afraid you've already missed your time slot."

I feel a soft but sudden nudge at my skirt. My heart jumps to my throat as I look down. It's a golden-haired dog with a red bandanna around its neck. I shrink behind my case, thrusting it between the dog and me.

"He won't hurt you," the dark-skinned girl says as she jumps from her chair. She holds the dog back by the collar.

I can't breathe. Didn't Mother Dee say the outsiders trained their dogs to attack us?

"He's just curious," the girl says.

I look to Tanner for help, but he's not paying attention to me. He's still talking with the woman and pointing to her list. The dog tries to approach again, but the girl seems to have a good hold on him this time.

"You sure he won't attack?" I ask, my voice shaking.

She nods and draws the dog behind her body. Then, she points to my case. "You play the violin?"

"How'd you—" And then I stop myself, realizing I'm still holding my violin case as a shield. My cheeks warm.

She smiles. "Me too. Name's Talia."

"Gentry," I say, slowly returning my case to my side.

"What are you going to play?"

From the corner of my eye, I spot Tanner shaking his head in frustration. I loosen the hold on my case a little and shift from foot to foot. "Uh, we were going to play 'Gold Rush.'"

Talia cocks her head to the side. "Never heard of it. Is it country or something?"

"Bluegrass," I say.

She nods. "That's cool." The panting dog peeks around Talia's hip; she pets its head. "You're lucky." Talia gives the woman behind the table a stern look, and I begin to see the resemblance between them. "My mom made me play boring classical. She said that's what people expected."

"Really?" I ask, a wave of nausea rolling over me. Maybe it's a good thing we're too late to play.

Talia ruffles the scruff of hair along her dog's neck. "Anyway, this gentle beast is Rockstar." On cue, Rockstar sits on his hind legs next to her. "You want to pet him?"

I shake my head, hard.

"I can't believe this," I hear Tanner saying to Talia's mom.

Talia inches closer with Rockstar. "Aw, come on. I promise he won't bite. Just lift your hand a little more and let him sniff you first."

"You sure he won't bite?" I ask. She nods. I press my lips together and lower my case, setting it on the ground. Immediately, Rockstar nudges my trembling hand with his wet nose. Talia giggles.

The dog's moist breath tickles my palm. I smile and carefully pet the top of Rockstar's head.

He licks my hand. I jump back slightly.

Talia laughs again. "That's just a kiss. I knew he liked you."

I carefully pet Rockstar's soft coat again. Long strokes along his back. And sides. This isn't so bad. My heartbeat slows.

"We've come all this way," my brother says loudly to Talia's mom, yanking my attention away from Rockstar's golden hair. Tanner looks defeated. "You don't understand. This is my sister's dream."

Talia juts out her hip. Her hand lands right on it. "Mom, seriously?"

Talia's mom shakes her head at her daughter. My heart speeds up again. If I talked to one of my mothers that way, especially Mother Lenora, I'd be punished. No questions asked.

"Let the kids play," Talia says.

But her mom doesn't jump up and strike her. Instead, she leans back in her chair with a sigh. "We were going to take a break after the quartet anyway. I guess you can go on when they finish." She holds up a finger. "But only one song."

I shake my head. "That's okay, we don't have to play."

Tanner's smile widens. "Thank you so much."

Talia pulls on Rockstar with a nod and looks to me. "You can do it."

"Better hurry," Talia's mom instructs. "Sounds like they're wrapping it up. Go to the bottom of the ramp, and the emcee will introduce you when they're ready for you."

My brother snatches his case and then gets mine.

"Nice meeting you," Talia says, giving Rockstar another pet on his head.

I turn to see Tanner, already near the base of the ramp. "You too," I say and hurry after him.

"Gentry," Talia calls.

I stop and look back at her.

"I like your costume," she says pointing and then gives me a thumbs-up. "It's really cool."

Costume? I look down, and then realize she's talking about my dress. My face flushes with embarrassment.

"Good luck," she says with a smile.

My stomach turns. She thinks I'm wearing a costume.

The quartet finishes, and applause erupts from the crowd of outsiders. I meet Tanner at the base of the ramp that leads to the stage.

What were we thinking? "We can't do this," I say to my brother as he's tuning his instrument.

"What?" he shouts over the clapping.

My hands clench the sides of my long skirt. "They're expecting classical music."

Tanner dramatically rolls his eyes and twists the fine tuner for his E string.

"We're not good enough. There's a ton of people, and they'll all be staring at us."

My brother finishes tuning. "Yeah. So?"

I sigh. "Talia thinks I'm wearing a costume."

My brother chuckles under his breath and lowers his instrument.

"It's not funny," I say, crossing my arms over my chest.

Tanner tucks his violin under his arm. "We've been talking about this forever, right?"

I nod.

"And we're finally here, aren't we?"

"I know, but I didn't think it would be like this."

Tanner shakes his head. "Gentry, sometimes you have to push yourself—and maybe even get uncomfortable—to get what you want."

A man with a white beard appears behind Tanner. "How should I introduce you two?"

I jump at the sound of his voice.

"We're the Forrester Duet," Tanner says to the emcee and then turns to me. "Right?"

The emcee's shoes pound up the ramp before I can respond.

My arms drop to my sides. "What if we're not good enough?"

"We are." He points to my violin case on the ground. "You are." The emcee makes the announcement, and Tanner glances back to see if I'm following.

My heart races. I bend to get my violin and quickly tune it. He's already at the microphone by the time I slowly step onto the gray-planked stage. The crowd politely applauds. Talia is right up front. The rest of the outsiders surround the front and sides of the stage. The emcee stands behind us on the ramp. My chest tightens.

"You coming?" Tanner whispers. He's already tucked his violin under his chin. I gulp and approach the second microphone. Overhead, the rust-colored roof seems to press down on us. Outsiders are all around us. We're trapped.

My brother clears his throat. It reverberates through the

speakers and across the Plaza. The audience shifts, looking suddenly uneasy.

"This is 'Gold Rush,'" he says, his voice cracking on the last word.

My violin quivers in my hands. My bow knocks the microphone stand. I spot a blond girl in the crowd and try to envision my sister Amy. I lift my violin to my chin. My hands are shaking so hard, I let my bow hover above the string, instead of correctly on it. I don't want to accidentally make a sound too early.

The crowd has gone silent. I can hear the fry bread popping and expanding in hot oil. Skirt steaks sizzle on a nearby griddle and smoke fills the air.

With a breath, my brother lifts his head and plays the introductory notes. Almost too late, I join him on the downbeat of the second measure. The tempo's so quick, there's no time to think. We race and lilt, echoing each other's melody. I close my eyes and can feel Tanner's foot taps through the floorboards. And suddenly, it's like we're home. I hear the claps of the audience, keeping time.

My fingertips hurry across the fingerboard, not missing a single double-stop. We slow to allegro only briefly for the middle section of the piece and then speed up again. I can sense people on their feet now. Dancing. Clapping. Twirling.

I open my eyes to Tanner's smile, right before we end on the harmonic note.

The applause is sudden. Talia jumps up and down. She places her fingers between her lips and whistles. People scream for an encore. Tanner takes a bow. I lower my violin. And then, I can't help it: I bow. The applause grows louder. My cheeks already hurt from smiling.

When I stand upright, from the edge of my vision, I spot the familiar red hair. Crossing the Plaza and moving toward us. My smile drops.

It's Father.

6.

I squirm in the back seat of Tanner's pickup. Father's driving. Tanner's in the front passenger seat, sulking next to him. The silence is unbearable.

After he found us, Father bought lunch off one of the vendors and then ordered us inside Tanner's truck to eat. I tasted nothing.

Father has said nothing. In fact, nobody has said anything. For hours.

Now he's driving us through the mountains on the High Road to Taos. Cars zip past as we putter along at a steady forty miles per hour. I dare a peek into the rearview mirror, hoping to catch some clue as to what Father's thinking, but his green eyes concentrate on the road ahead, revealing nothing.

By the time we finally reach the town of Taos, I begin to wonder whether we're ever going to stop.

"Father?" Tanner shifts in his seat, breaking the silence.

I try to breathe. Yes, finally. Tanner will talk to Father and make this better.

"If you're gonna kill us, can we just get it over with?" my brother snaps.

Wait. Who said anything about killing us?

Tanner points angrily to the dashboard clock. "We've been driving for hours."

Father's face reddens, but still he says nothing. His knuckles go white as he turns west, blinding us with the sun.

Tanner lowers his visor, but Father squints against the blazing brightness and speeds up. My stomach twists around my tasteless lunch. What have we done? What if I don't get to say good-bye to Amy? Mother? All because we had to play in the festival.

I wish Father would yell at us. Something. Anything would be better than these miles and miles of silence.

And then I see it. Up ahead. A giant drop-off. Father slows as we approach the steel bridge that stretches over the massive gorge and pulls over.

This is it: We're dead.

"Get out," Father says as he kills the engine. He jumps from the truck and slams the door. Through the bug-splattered windshield, I see him walk away from us, moving farther and farther across the long bridge.

"Where are we?" I whisper, even though I know there's no way Father can hear.

Tanner glances over the seat for the first time since we left Santa Fe. Confusion lines his forehead. "No idea."

"What are we doing here?"

Tanner shakes his head. "I don't know that, either."

I can hardly even see Father now. He's a dot on the burning horizon.

My brother turns and pushes his door open before jumping out. "He wants us out. Let's get out."

I clench my jaw and force myself to slide across the seat before jumping out of Tanner's truck. Immediately, the hot wind gusts across the gorge, whipping my dress against my legs. A long strand of hair escapes my braid. I pull it from my mouth and tuck it behind my ear, fighting the wind to match Tanner's pace.

Soon, we find Father, alone on the bridge. His red hair glints in the sunlight as he peers over the edge. We stand on either side of him, and for the first time, I look down. The tops of two sheer cliffs support the ends of the bridge. The river runs hundreds of feet below us.

I wrap my arms around myself.

"Father?" Tanner asks, his voice softer now.

For the first time today, Father looks at us. Really looks at us. "Your grandfather brought me here when I was younger," he says, like a sudden calm has settled over him. "It's the Rio Grande Gorge."

My shoulders relax a little at the sound of his voice. At least he's talking. I glance at the Rio Grande, raging far below us.

"He took me here only once," Father says, his voice carried away by the wind. He pulls a handkerchief from his pocket and wipes the sweat from his forehead. "When I wanted to leave the community."

My jaw drops; my eyes move away from the deep hole to his tired face. I never knew my father wanted to leave Watchful.

"You never told me you wanted to leave," Tanner says, the shock evident in his voice.

Father nods, returning his handkerchief to his pocket. "I'm not proud of it."

"So why then?" I ask, my voice unsure. "Why would Grandfather take you here?"

Father looks at the hole splitting the earth. "To show me the power of God." Another rush of wind lifts the hair around my face. Hot. Like the breath of God.

Father's hands grip the bridge's railing. "Hundreds of years ago, a boy wanted to leave his family and venture out into the world. Even though God repeatedly told him to stay, the boy went anyway."

I glance at Tanner. He shifts, uneasily.

"The boy had only been gone a few days when he became homesick and decided to return to his family. But when he reached this place, God appeared before him. Angry that the boy had defied Him, God struck the earth with His staff and split it in two. The staff left a huge hole in the earth." My gaze travels the gorge that splits the earth for miles. "The boy had no way to cross. Separated from his family, he died all alone."

"How did you know?" Tanner asks. "How did you know we'd left Watchful?"

Father sighs. "You think I don't know the heart of my own son?" He turns away from the railing and gives my brother a stern look. "The Prophet has forbidden Gentry from leaving the community. Therefore, I forbid it." He shakes his head. "You *knew* this."

My brother's shoulders sink.

"But, Father," I say. "It wasn't his—"

He puts a hand up, stopping me.

But I *wanted* to go.

"It's indefensible, Gentry. You defied the word of God."

The threat of tears is sudden. "I didn't think—"

"That's right," Father says. "You didn't think. Neither of you did."

Had we really defied God? I really didn't mean to. I just wanted to play my violin so badly. But what if I can't return to my family now? To Amy? What would I do? "I'm sorry, Father," I say, a tear running down my cheek. "We both are. Aren't we, Tanner?"

But my brother doesn't look sorry. His face is red. His lips clamp shut.

Father wipes the tear from my face and sighs. "We will await nightfall before we return home."

I manage to breathe.

He lifts a finger. "This one time only."

"Thank you, Father," I say, wanting to hug him. I know I shouldn't, so my hands clasp the railing instead.

Tanner remains silent as Father picks up a rock from the bridge and pitches it over the edge. It falls for what seems like forever until I detect a tiny splash in the river. Father shakes his head. "Let's only hope God allows it."

***

It's been dark for a few hours by the time we return to the familiar foothills, north of Santa Fe. Everyone will be in their family homes by now, so Father thinks we should be able to sneak inside undetected.

As Father drives, Tanner leans his head against the passenger-side window. I think he's pretending to be asleep.

I finally get the courage to ask: "What about our mothers?" I know they probably realized I was gone around dinnertime when I wasn't there to help.

Father twists the ring on his left finger, the one he's worn since he married Mother Lenora. At least, that's what Mother told me. "I lied to them," he says, his voice barely a whisper.

I lean forward slightly so I can hear.

"I told them you'd fallen at school, and I had to take you into town for an X-ray. I told them, while I was there, I might as well get my truck serviced and catch a ride home from Tanner." He glances back at me through the rearview mirror. "I forbid them to say a word to anyone."

I fall against my seat, feeling guilty all over again. Father lied for me. I defied God, and my father lied to our mothers. All because I wanted to play my violin.

"Let me do the talking when we get home, okay?" he adds.

"Yes, Father," I say.

"Tanner?" Father asks, touching my brother's shoulder. "You aren't going to give me any trouble, are you?"

Tanner shrugs away from Father's hand.

With a sigh, Father slows as we approach the concrete wall that surrounds our community. "If they're at the gate, remember to let me do the talking."

My heart speeds up as I nod.

Father uses a clicker to open the gate. I hold my breath as it slowly creaks open to . . . more darkness.

I breathe. Nobody's there. Not even Buckley. I can sense Father's relief, too, as he drives us into the compound. Gravel crunches beneath our tires.

We turn right to take the long way around the meeting-house when, from out of nowhere, a black truck with oversize tires appears in the road and cuts us off. Our tires skid to a stop. My fingers dig into the edge of the seat. It has to be Buckley. Light suddenly floods the back of our truck. Tanner bolts upright and turns to see. Another truck blocks us from behind. I freeze. It's the God Squad.

Buckley jumps from his rig, holding a shotgun even though he has a handgun strapped to his hip. "Get out of the truck!" he shouts.

Tanner's eyes go wide.

"Father?" I say, my voice shaking.

"Do what they say. Everything will be fine."

Father and Tanner pile out. There's four God Squad, dressed in black, standing at attention in a line in front of Tanner's truck. Each wears a badge, and their straw cowboy hats shadow their slender faces. The fifth one is Buckley. Holding his shot-gun, he also wears all black, but with a black felt cowboy hat that clings to his fat head.

My knees buckle when my feet hit the ground. I almost fall, but Tanner catches me. "I've got you," he says, and for a second, I feel a little better he's here.

Father moves toward them. "What seems to be the problem, gentlemen?"

"Conway," Uncle Max says, slipping from the shadows.

Buckley smiles with his crooked teeth. My heart stutters.

"There's an evil in your house." Uncle Max steps into the headlight's beam, making his skin look ghostly in the harsh light. His dark suit blends into the night.

"Pardon me?" Father asks, more high-pitched than normal.

"Since you've been unable to fulfill your duty as a man in this community, we're here to help." The Vulture signals one of the God Squad, who opens the door to the meetinghouse. The entire community bursts out through the opening and floods beneath the stars in a sea of pastel dresses and white button-down shirts. They gather, facing us.

My brothers and sisters are here. My mothers, too.

I find Mother in the middle of our family. Baby Bill sleeps in her arms. She glances at me and then averts her eyes with shame. My face flushes hot. Amy yawns as she treads behind her. And then, there's Meryl's glare, matching everyone else's.

Father approaches Uncle Max and lowers his voice, "I'm sure we can discuss this in private."

The Vulture caws. "Yes, I'm sure that would be easier on you, wouldn't it?"

From the light of Tanner's truck, I can see the veins bulge in Father's neck.

Uncle Max turns on his heel, kicking up a cloud of dust that floats through the beam of light. "But the community must bear witness to what happens to those who defy the Prophet." With a scowl on his pale face, the Vulture struts toward Tanner and me.

I step backward, but there's nowhere to go. The rest of the God Squad shuffle in behind us, blocking us—now there are eight in all—their weapons ready. I clutch Tanner's rigid arm.

Uncle Max's beady eyes narrow and focus on my brother. "This is not the first time you have defied the Prophet."

What?

"The Prophet is familiar with your refusal."

What? What's he talking about?

"Hannah Forrester," Uncle Max calls into the night.

Father tries to pull Uncle Max aside. "This is between you and me, Max."

Buckley cocks his gun, aiming it at my father.

My heart skyrockets.

"Back away," Buckley commands, his voice gruff.

Father releases him and slowly puts his hands up, doing as he's told.

Uncle Max pulls out a handkerchief and wipes the place Father touched. He looks to the crowd. "Hannah, come here."

My mother gives Meryl the baby and bows her head as she approaches the Vulture.

I sense Tanner's fist clench next to me.

Uncle Max drops the handkerchief into Mother's waiting hands. He clears his throat, so everyone can hear. "A priesthood mother must raise her children to be virtuous and good." He turns to Mother, but her gaze remains fixed on the handkerchief. "Your son has strayed."

Mother suddenly looks up and shakes her head, fear rising in her eyes.

Uncle Max faces the crowd. "This boy is no longer welcome in this community."

Tanner trembles.

"He's an apostate."

I can't breathe. An apostate spends the afterlife in the lowest realm of hell. He can never live among God's chosen again.

Tanner's shoulders shake.

"No," my mother cries as she looks at my father.

"The Prophet has spoken," Uncle Max says.

"Thanks be to God," the community responds.

What? "No!" I shout.

"Gentry," Father warns.

"But it's my fault!" I say. "*I* wanted to play in the festival."

Grumbles ripple through the crowd.

My fingers slip from Tanner's arm as I turn and address Uncle Max. "Please. You can't do this. He only did it because I asked him to."

Sharp gasps pepper the air.

"Yes," Uncle Max says, his beady eyes narrowing. "You left to play the devil's music, didn't you?"

My fingernails dig into my palms. "It's *not* the devil's music."

Uncle Max clucks his tongue at Father. "I see you've still failed to teach your daughter how to give proper respect." His head swivels on his neck until his glare lands on me. "Perhaps she needs a better teacher."

From the corner of my eye, I see Amy slump against Meryl. Suddenly, I realize I'm letting the evil inside me show again. "I'm sorry," I say, trying to keep sweet like I'm supposed to, hoping to save Tanner. But I'm too late.

"Hannah, take Gentry home," Father barks.

My gaze jumps to my brother. He looks lost.

Mother grabs my arm; I yank away. "We can't leave him," I plead. "Where will he go? He has no one out there."

My mother's eyes dart between the stares of judgment. "That's not our concern."

I point to Tanner. "But he's your son."

"Come home. Now," Mother says, firm. The firmest I've ever heard her speak to me.

Father won't meet my pleading eyes. But the rest of the community won't look away, transfixed, seeing our family drama play out, bit by painful bit.

I turn away from their curious stares. "It's my fault," I argue again and move toward Uncle Max, desperate to explain. "You can't do this to Tanner when it's not his fault." The God Squad blocks me before I get too close. Their fingers snatch my biceps, preventing me from going anywhere. I struggle in their grasp, but it only tightens. "Punish me instead."

"Gentry," Tanner says. He tries to approach, but the God Squad won't let him get any closer.

Why'd I let go of his arm? I should have held on tight and never let go.

"I'm leaving," he says, his voice resigned.

No, he can't. I feel the tears stinging the backs of my eyes.

"Open the gate," Uncle Max shouts, and the hinges groan in the distance as the gate opens once more.

Tanner pops open the rear of his pickup to retrieve his

violin case. He turns to me with a weak smile. "For what it's worth, I had fun."

"Me too," I whisper, even though I know I'm supposed to stay quiet.

I follow Tanner as close as the God Squad will let me. I watch my brother's back as he walks through the gate, his violin case swaying in his right hand.

The gate closes behind him. Tears flow down my cheeks, but I don't dare blink. I don't want to stop seeing my brother.

From out of nowhere, Mother places a hand on the small of my back. "Come on home," she says, her voice calm. Too calm.

The gate closes with a final clang, separating my brother from me. Like a deep, wide gorge.

I whip around to face her. Father's there, too. "I'm the one who wasn't supposed to leave, but I did. Why didn't you punish me instead?"

"We will," Father grunts.

I shake my head. What's wrong with him? Both of them? "Don't you even care what happens to him?"

"You must forget your brother," Mother says, her voice distant. "He's dead to us now."

7.

Anger and sadness weigh me down like a pair of buckets, brimming with water. My parents say I should forget about Tanner. They say he's a son of perdition, a sinner who won't take part in the glory of the afterlife. But he's my brother. He's our family. And he should be here with us now.

How will he survive out there all alone? Tanner has no food. No water. No money. Nobody but the coyotes to keep him company. What if he starves to death? Or worse?

It's all my fault. If only I hadn't gone to the festival, Tanner would still be here.

My stomach rumbles, but I barely feel the hunger anymore. Uncle Max ordered Father to control his family, or else.

I don't even know what that means, but I've been locked in the upstairs room I share with Meryl and Amy for the last three days without food. It would almost be bearable if Amy would talk to me when she comes in each night. But she hasn't spoken to me since I returned from Santa Fe.

She's sprawled across our bed in her nightgown, belly down, her chin resting on her arms. Amy stares off into space as her record player spins the same Elvis record for at least the thousandth time. A couple of years ago, Tanner saved enough money to buy the player for her at the Tesuque flea market. It's her absolute favorite possession, the one thing that's truly hers.

"Suspicious Minds" starts again, the needle popping and skipping the same line at the beginning of the song.

It's only the two of us in here until Meryl finishes her nightly chores. I sit on Meryl's bed and will Amy to look at me. But she's as still as a deer that senses a predator nearby.

"You want to talk about it?" I ask her again.

She doesn't respond.

"I don't understand why you won't talk to me."

My sister rolls to her side, away from me, and faces the record player.

Elvis bellows another verse, and I shift, uneasy. Meryl's bed creaks beneath me. "You can't stay quiet forever."

Nothing.

My face flushes. I jump from the bed and cross the room to the record player. I rip the needle from the record; it makes a scratching sound.

"Hey!" Amy says and sits up.

"So you *can* talk."

Her neck flushes red. "Turn it back on."

I shake my head. "Not until you tell me why you're mad at me."

Amy crosses her arms over her chest, covering the pink flowers Mother needlepointed onto her nightgown.

"I'm the one who's being punished here," I say softly. "I don't know why you're so mad." Though, I really do. It's my fault we'll never see Tanner again.

Amy pushes her fingers under her glasses and sniffles, making me feel like the jerk I am.

"I'm sorry," I say, regretting how fiercely I'd lashed out at her. "I really am."

Her hands drop to her lap. She levels me with a glare through smudged glasses. "You lied to me," she says.

"I did not," I say, suddenly defensive again. I'd given her a lot of good reasons to be mad at me, but lying certainly wasn't one of them.

"Uh-huh," Amy says, sounding a little out of breath now. "You left."

I shake my head, not understanding.

"You said you'd never leave me." She sucks in a long breath. "Never. Ever. That's what you said."

Then, I get it: She thought I'd abandoned her. Suddenly I can't breathe too great, either.

"When Uncle Max said you'd left, I thought—he was lying," she says, her face turning the color of her neck.

I slowly approach her.

"I told—him you would never do that."

I was wrong: I'm worse than a jerk. While I was having fun with Tanner, Amy was defending me to the Vulture. I carefully place my palm between her shoulder blades, attempting to calm her. "You stuck up for me?" I ask.

Amy shrugs away from my touch. "Yeah." She gulps a breath. "Won't do that again."

I drop to the bed, sitting next to her. The edge of the mattress sags beneath our combined weight. When her breathing becomes steadier, I continue, "I'm so sorry."

She gives me a sideways glance.

"All this time, I thought you were mad at me because of Tanner."

"I am," she says, her voice tight.

I smile slightly. "You should be."

Amy gives a firm nod.

I sigh. "I really didn't mean to hurt you. I was just so excited to play in the festival." I hesitate for a second and then reach for her hand. "I'd understand if you want to be mad at me forever."

Though my sister doesn't look at me, her warm fingers squeeze mine, pushing out some of the sadness.

The bolt on our door clicks. We both startle; I release her hand. Father opens the door for Meryl. His green eyes zero in on mine, and the anger and sadness fill me all over again. How could he? How could he stand there and let Uncle Max throw Tanner out of Watchful?

I turn away from him with a huff. The mattress creaks.

"You don't have any right to be upset with me," he says, which only makes me angrier.

I jump from the bed. "No *right*? At least I *tried* to talk Uncle Max into letting Tanner stay."

Father shakes his head. "There was no point."

Every muscle tightens. "How do you know that? You didn't even try!"

"Careful," Meryl says. "He's your priesthood head."

"Says the perfect daughter," I say, glaring at her. "You're just jealous of Tanner and me. You always have been."

"Gentry," Father barks. "There are things you do not understand."

My hands clench, defensive. "I understand plenty. Tanner's my brother and you let him go." I snap my fingers. "Just like that, and you're not even upset that he's gone."

"Quiet." Father says it so loud, it's frightening. Amy clutches her pillow to her chest. He jabs his finger toward me. "These feelings are of the devil. You must focus on your family."

Meryl wipes her eyes, and suddenly I feel bad all over again. I shouldn't have yelled at her, either.

"If I *had* said more," Father says, "I'd be going against the Prophet." He swallows hard. "And then, I'd risk losing you, too." He gestures around the room and outside the door. "*All* of you."

"Why would you lose us?" I ask, suddenly nervous.

"It's none of your concern," he says, brushing away my question as usual. "You must keep sweet and focus on abolishing the evil inside." He takes a calming breath and then approaches, leaning over to kiss the top of my head. Ordinarily, I'd welcome the rare show of affection from him, but I'm still angry and confused. I twist away.

Father returns to the doorway. "I only pray that someday you'll have the maturity to understand why I did what I did."

My muscles are in a million knots. "How much longer are you going to keep me in here?"

"Until you realize you cannot go against the Prophet," he says and then shuts the door. The lock clicks.

I turn to Meryl. She's still wiping her eyes. I sigh my frustration. I've made a real mess of things. "I didn't mean—"

"Yes, you did." She pulls two slices of bread from the pockets of her dress. "Here," she says.

94

I glance at the locked door, knowing I'm not supposed to eat. Knowing she knows I'm not supposed to eat. She places the bread in my hand. Immediately, my mouth waters.

Why would the perfect daughter sneak me food? I shouldn't eat it, but I'm too hungry to resist. I take a bite of Mother Lenora's bread. Nutty and delicious.

"I'll try to sneak you more in the morning," Meryl says, her voice quiet.

I stop chewing. "Why would you do that?" I ask through the crumbs.

"Because I agree with you," she whispers. "Father should've done more." She glances between Amy and me. "But, if either of you repeat that, I'll deny it." She turns to the chest of drawers we all share and opens the top drawer to retrieve her nightgown. "Just tell me one thing."

I shove the second piece of bread into my mouth and nod.

"Were you scared?"

"To play in the festival?" I ask through a mouthful of bread.

She wads her gown between her hands. "No, I mean were you scared out there?"

"I was at first," I admit. But then, I think of Talia and her mom. The crowd cheering for us. Even Rockstar, Talia's dog. They weren't anything like I expected. "Then, it was the most wonderful thing ever. Nobody was there to tell me how to think or feel. For the first time, I got to decide." I stop, realizing it all probably sounds silly to her.

Without a word, Meryl nods and then turns toward the wall to put on her nightgown.

***

Unfamiliar shouts outside our bedroom door awaken me to the darkness. Heavy stomps approach. Beside me, Amy doesn't move. I sit upright in bed as the door bursts open, splitting the wood along the doorframe.

Meryl screams from her bed. Someone flips on the light. It's two men, dressed in black: the God Squad.

Adrenaline shoots through my body. I yank the sheet to my chest. Amy remains still.

"What's going on?" I ask, but they don't answer. It's Buckley with his bright red face and one other goon. He starts opening drawers, pulling out clothes, and throwing them on the floor.

Amy jerks the blanket over her head and trembles, making the whole mattress shake.

"Father," I call, my bare feet hitting the carpet as I try to remember what night it is. Yes, it's his night to stay in Mother's room next door. "Mother."

Within seconds, Father appears in the doorway with his

red hair sticking out in all directions and a shadow of stubble across his cheeks. His tired eyes go wide when he sees the men. "What's going on here?"

"Off the bed," Buckley grunts at Amy. She doesn't move. "Off," he says, poking the lump on our bed with his black stick.

Father steps inside our room. "Let her at least wake up."

Amy reaches for her glasses on the nightstand. Buckley raises his stick, as if preparing to break her arm.

I hold out my hands to stop him. "She needs her glasses to see."

His glare flicks to the nightstand, where my sister's thick glasses sit, and then returns to me. For a second, I think he's going to strike me instead.

"I'll check over here," the other man says as he opens the accordion doors to our closet.

Buckley lowers his stick, and in one motion, Amy snatches her glasses, scoots across the mattress toward me, and stands. She stumbles into my arms, whimpering against my chest.

Buckley wastes no time in flipping our mattress, trapping Meryl against the wall. There's nothing but dust bunnies between the box springs and mattress.

Father smooths his hair against his head. "Is there something we can help you find?"

Mother's ashen face appears behind his. She's wearing a

half-tied robe over her gown. "It's the middle of the night." Baby Bill's crying in her arms. "Can this not wait until sunrise?"

Buckley squats, the fabric of his slacks growing tight like sausage casings around his heavy thighs. He slides his hand under the box springs. Amy buries her face in my shoulder.

"Found it," the other one says, pulling my violin case from our closet.

My heart jumps to my throat. Amy squeaks like I've squeezed her too hard.

Buckley rises.

"My daughter's violin?" Father asks. "Why would you want her violin?"

"We're under orders to search the house. Get your wives and children outside." The man uses my violin case to point to the door and clumsily knocks it against the wall.

"Careful," I say.

Buckley aims his stick at me. "We're searching for the devil's things." By now, my other brothers and sisters are outside our bedroom door. Kate's and Kel's eyes fill with fear. We're all hiding something forbidden: an old comic book; a cartoon movie; a favorite CD. Even Meryl has a plastic heart bracelet she sometimes wears hidden under her sleeve.

Mother Lenora shoves Kel and Kate aside. She's dressed. Her hair's done in a perfect braid. As if she's been awake for hours.

Mother's eyes narrow. "Did you know they were coming and fail to tell the rest of us, Lenora?"

"Come, children," Mother Lenora orders, completely ignoring my mother's question.

My brothers and sisters start moving, trailed by a yawning Mother Dee in her pale nightgown. Her hand rests on her rounded belly as she walks away. Within seconds, their bare feet thud down the stairs.

"Conway?" Mother says, her voice unsure. Baby Bill squirms and suckles her fingers.

"It's all right," Father says. "Go with the others. I'll figure this out." He gestures us outside. "You too, girls. Downstairs."

But I'm not leaving. Not without my violin. I shake my head in response.

Father's jaw tightens.

A pale hand grasps his shoulder from behind. Father spins around, as if ready to fight.

"Conway," Uncle Max says in a disarming voice. The Vulture's dressed in his black suit and looks freshly shaven.

He really shouldn't be here. The God Squad shouldn't be here. No man is supposed to see us like this with our hair down and in our nightgowns. No man but Father has ever been inside our room.

Yet Father steps aside.

The Vulture smooths his suit as he lifts his shoulders with authority and enters our bedroom. He clears his throat. "The Prophet calls."

"Thanks be to God," Meryl and Amy uniformly say like a pair of robots.

Uncle Max seems to realize Meryl is hidden behind the tossed mattress. His lips twist into a smile. "Thanks, indeed. The Prophet has had a revelation: We need to purge the evil threatening our community."

"I don't understand," Father says.

The Vulture looks down his nose at my father. "And that's precisely the problem here, Conway. The Prophet sees his people taking on the evil spirit of the outside world through forbidden books, movies." Uncle Max turns to me with a raised eyebrow. "Music."

My arms fall slack, away from Amy. "You can't be serious."

"You *dare* disrespect me?" he says between clenched teeth.

"That's three more days in your room, young lady," Father barks.

My gaze whips around to his red face. Whose side is he on?

Uncle Max clucks his tongue. "Conway, you're losing control here. This girl clearly needs stronger discipline."

Father grips the broken doorframe.

"The Prophet has tolerated this music, because you said it makes Hannah more docile."

Docile?

"But things are clearly out of hand." He opens his pasty hand and then snatches it shut. "Give them a crumb, and they'll take the loaf."

"I don't want the loaf," I argue, even though I know I shouldn't say anything. Music's the only thing I'm allowed that lets me be me. Now he wants to take it away? I desperately eye my violin case in the man's hand. "What about the hymns we sing?" I ask, hoping to sound more confident than I feel. "That's music."

"True," Amy says, and then hums "Love One Another."

Even though I'm flattered she's defending me, I wish she wouldn't. I don't want to get her into trouble, too.

Uncle Max's face warps, like he's tasted something sour. I can feel Buckley and the other goon watching, as if waiting for the order to attack. Amy keeps humming.

"Stop," Father says.

I nudge her, and the music stops. She looks hurt.

The Vulture's expression tightens. "Are you telling me you defied the Prophet in order to play our sacred hymns at this festival?"

I press my lips together. He knows that's not what I mean.

Uncle Max lets out a dry laugh. "Admit it. You left to play the devil's music."

"Bluegrass isn't the devil's music," I argue. "It's just—"

"What?" he prods. "What is it?"

"Music. Same as our hymns."

"And you're qualified to make that determination?" He nears, hovering over me with those probing eyes. "The Prophet speaks to *you*?"

Buckley slaps his stick against his palm.

I flinch and glance at Father, but he only shakes his head. I wish he'd say something as my priesthood head. Or even better, as my father. But he stands motionless, like he did with Tanner, letting the Vulture peck away at me until there's nothing left.

Suddenly, the mattress drops away from the wall and returns to our bed frame. Meryl must've pushed it. I'd forgotten she was even there.

The distraction breaks Uncle Max's cold glare; the God Squad jumps to attention.

"What if she promises not to play?" Meryl asks, clutching her quilt to her chest. She shifts her weight from foot to foot. "Wouldn't it take more discipline if her violin's still here to tempt her? Wouldn't *that* be the more faithful response?"

Wait, is she doing what I think she is? Is she actually trying to *help* me?

Uncle Max smiles, slipping into my sister's snare.

Meryl lowers her gaze. The Prophet teaches a woman's hair is sacred. We never cut it, so we can use it to wash our husband's feet in heaven. And Meryl's hair is the most beautiful in Watchful. It falls in a long golden cascade over her shoulder and down past her waist.

"Conway," the Vulture says. "Your daughter may be on to something."

Father suddenly looks uneasy. For a second, I could swear Meryl smiles behind her hair. But that notion fades as quickly as it appears.

The Vulture turns to the goon with my violin case and flaps his arm at him. "Leave it."

Amy claps her hands.

"Thank you, Uncle Max," I say, putting my hand over hers, trying to conceal her enthusiasm.

The man places my case on our messy bed.

Uncle Max is still looking at Meryl. "You will report to me immediately if she tries to play this instrument?"

"I'll report it," Father says.

Meryl looks up shyly and nods.

The Vulture's thin lips curl into a smile. "I will check with you weekly to make sure she's abiding by her punishment."

Uncle Max snaps his fingers at the God Squad. "You overlooked something," he says as he nears Meryl.

Buckley's bloodshot eyes dart around the room.

Meryl's cheeks go pale. And then I see: Her plastic bracelet peeks from beneath her sleeve. It's too late for her to cover it.

The Vulture seems to notice the bracelet, but then he turns toward the God Squad. "The record player must go," Uncle Max orders, ripping the plug from the wall.

What?

"But that's mine!" Amy cries.

"Yes, and you can thank your sister for its absence," he says, wrapping the cord around the player.

My stomach churns as he passes off Amy's prized possession.

The Vulture wipes his long fingers on a white handkerchief, leaving lines of dust on the cloth. "If we hadn't had this little chat about the violin," he says with a cruel grin, "I never would have seen your record player."

8.

I haven't heard from Tanner. It's been three months since Uncle Max kicked him out of Watchful, and even longer since he forced our friend Channing into hiding. And now our house is too quiet.

There are plenty of us left, but Tanner's absence has left a gaping hole in our family. There's no more laughter. No more pranks. No music.

Mother says I should keep sweet and forget about my brother, but that only makes the gap between us feel wider. That, plus the fact that I haven't played my violin since the festival.

On top of it all, Uncle Max hasn't stopped checking up on me. The Vulture has swooped in every week for the official report from Meryl. It's always the same: *No, my sister hasn't played her violin.* Yet his visits seem to last longer and longer. He even stayed for dinner last week when Meryl cooked.

Thank goodness I didn't have to sit at the same table, but I could overhear him cawing the Prophet's revelation that something evil looms over God's chosen—a sign that the end of the world is near.

The Prophet wants us to be prepared. So now, Uncle Max insists the girls join the boys for survival class. I stand next to Kel on the outer edge of a cluster of kids my age. The dry November chill seeps through my cardigan, through my dress, and into my skin. I rub my arms to keep warm, but don't dare move closer to the fire. Not with Dirk there, cooking worms in a frying pan over the fire he built from scraps of wood.

The white scars on his hand glisten as he flips the worms. Father told me he got the scars from a snakebite when he was a baby, and when Dirk survived and the snake died, the Prophet said it was proof of his son's divine lineage. I think it's proof Dirk is more poisonous than any snake.

Some of the girls pretend they're interested in what he's doing and elbow for a spot closer to the fire, but I know it's only because they have a crush on the Prophet's son. I have no idea why. He's as ugly as sin and as mean as a cougar caught in the rain.

Some of the kids around me turn green as the worms writhe and pop in the hot pan. My nose twists from the sickening smell that drifts along the breeze. Kate shoves her way between Kel and me, bending behind a sage bush to vomit. Then another girl peels away and does the same thing.

My stomach takes a queasy turn. If eating crispy worms is what it's going to take to survive the apocalypse with Dirk, I'd rather starve.

"And that's how it's done," he says, selecting a burnt one from the pan with his bare fingers. He flings it into his mouth with a crunch and chews. And chews. And chews. Some of the girls turn away or cover their mouths, while the boys groan with disgust. Dirk smiles, bits of worm stuck to his front teeth, as he asks, "Who wants to try one?"

Heads shake around me. Without looking our direction, he shouts, "Kel, how about you?"

My half brother shifts between his feet. He's already the color of green chile stew. Everyone turns to look at him. His Adam's apple slowly slides up and down his throat. "Uh, that's okay. I'm not hungry."

I smile. Giggles spread throughout our cluster.

Dirk's face hardens. "You're not hungry?" The laughter dies as Dirk jumps to his feet. The group splits in two, allowing him to reach my half brother in a quick march. "Did you say you're not hungry?" He looms over Kel, who hasn't hit his growth spurt yet.

Kel's mouth drops open. Nothing comes out but an indecipherable moan.

"Answer me," Dirk says and, without warning, punches Kel in the eye—the sound of bone against bone.

I wince; my insides spin.

The swelling around Kel's eye is immediate; he sways and covers his face with shaky fingers.

Dirk raises his fist again. Kate quickly snatches my arm and squeezes.

"Because I know you must be hungry." Dirk smirks. "I know this because the Prophet cut your family's rations."

Some of the kids chuckle around us. My cheeks flush with embarrassment. The Prophet cut our meager food rations after casting out Tanner, saying they were being directed to more faithful families until further notice.

Dirk shoves Kel in the chest, making him stumble backward and fall to the ground. A cloud of dust swells around him.

Kate gasps in my ear. My throat tightens.

Dirk snatches Kel up by the shirt collar. "We'll see if *this* makes you hungry." Dirk's face is purple with rage as he drags my half brother uphill by his shirt. Pebbles slip beneath Kel's feet as he staggers. Some of them land nearby.

"Should we follow them?" one of the boys asks when they're about halfway up the hill. A couple of boys shrug. Others nod.

Kate's the first one to go. She makes her way uphill with determination. I lift my chin and follow my half sister. Her lavender skirt billows in the breeze, showing her thick socks beneath her skirt.

Soon, I hear the footsteps of others, the nervous chatter growing behind me with each step. The wind is stronger the higher we climb. I shiver and pull my sweater tight around me, trying to block the chill.

As we crest the hill, Kate stops in her tracks. I'm next behind her and jerk backward when I see. A brown mule deer has been tied to a piñon tree with thick ropes.

Dirk tosses Kel toward the animal. He lands on his knees with a heavy thud, careful to avoid the deer. She whisks her tail across her back as if warning him to stay away.

Soon everyone else reaches the top. Their jabbering immediately stops. The deer's ears flick with the newcomers.

Dirk slips a bowie knife from its holster and begins to pace, the blade glinting in the pale sunlight.

I bite my lip. The deer rears back. But it's no use. The rope is too tight.

"Time is short," Dirk grunts, pointing his knife at Kate's face. My heart thuds as she whimpers. "My father, *our* Prophet, says we must prepare. For the end of the world is near." He moves his blade away from Kate's face. She quickly wipes her cheeks. "Any day now, destruction will cover the earth, and only the righteous will be saved."

I immediately think of Tanner. He's an apostate now, who will be destroyed.

Kel is still hunched on the ground. Dirk crouches and waves the blade in front of his face. The deer's black nose twitches. Kel clutches his knees to his chest. I don't know who looks more scared: Kel or the deer.

"You must be prepared," Dirk repeats, facing us as he stands. Behind him, wolf-shaped clouds race across the open sky. "You must do whatever it takes in order to survive."

All of a sudden, Dirk spins around and jabs his knife toward Kel's chest. We gasp as the blade stops midair. Half of us clutch our chests. Dirk releases a vicious laugh. "Maybe you belong in hell with your apostate brother."

Kel vigorously shakes his head. "Please, no," he says, his voice weak.

I look at the scared faces of my classmates. No one dares make a sound. The piñon tree creaks in the breeze.

Dirk offers Kel the knife and lowers his voice. "You must prove you are worthy to live among God's chosen."

The deer huffs, like she knows what's about to happen. Her massive side shudders.

From the corner of my eye, I see silent tears running down

Kate's cheeks. Some of my classmates—both boys and girls—look sick all over again. Silent tension bumps between us.

What choice does Kel have? The Prophet teaches perfect obedience produces perfect faith. When it comes down to it, none of us want to be left behind. Even when it's Dirk telling you what to do.

Kel takes the knife in his trembling hand. The deer stomps her foot three times.

"Get up!" Dirk yells.

Kate blots her face with her sweater.

"Now!"

Kel manages to his feet, but his knees immediately buckle. He grasps the piñon tree to stay upright.

The deer snorts loudly, making us all jump.

Dirk runs his finger across the deer's throat in a single stroke. "There," he instructs coolly.

My half brother lifts the knife with both hands, like it's too heavy for him. Kate turns away. Most of the girls, and some of the boys, cover their eyes.

"What are you waiting for?" Dirk shouts, spittle shooting from his mouth.

The deer doesn't blink. Neither does Kel. A tear slips down his cheek.

"Do it!"

The blade glints as it moves. I shut my eyes at the last second.

The metallic smell of blood makes my stomach curdle. I hear a heavy thud, and the breeze carries Kel's whimper: "I'm sorry. I'm so, so sorry."

***

A few hours later, the rich smell of stew fills the kitchen. I'm washing dishes in the kitchen sink as Mother Dee places clear drinking glasses on the table. Her newborn daughter, Gwen, sleeps in a fabric sling across her middle.

"You're gonna spoil that child rotten," Mother Lenora warns as she stirs the large pot on the cooktop.

Mother Dee has barely put her baby down since she was born. "So what?" Mother Dee says.

I sense Mother Lenora tense behind me. "You plan on carrying all your babies around?"

"Maybe," Mother Dee says as she continues along the table. "God gave me two hands, so I don't see why not."

I smile to myself.

Mother walks into the kitchen, an empty laundry basket under her arm. "Have you seen Kel?"

My smile falls.

Mother Dee shakes her head and starts on the second table.

Mother turns her attention to Mother Lenora. "I was upstairs just now, and he's got this bruise around his eye."

Mother Lenora pinches dry herbs into the pot. She doesn't turn away from her stirring. "Clumsy boy probably fell again."

I flinch. That's what the adults always say when the kids show up with strange bruises.

"I'm not so sure," Mother says. "He's lying on his bed and won't say a word. The boys say he's been like that for hours."

I plunge my hands into the soapy water and scrub, scrub, scrub.

"Gentry, did something happen at school today?"

I shrug and keep washing.

"I think that spoon's clean," Mother says over my shoulder, and I realize I've been washing the same spoon over and over.

"Oh," I say and drop the spoon into the rinsing basin.

Her eyes narrow, like she knows I'm not telling her something. But then the house phone rings. Mother shakes her head and points to the living room. "Get Amy to help you slice the bread," she says and disappears downstairs to the basement. The ringing stops.

I dry my hands on a dish towel and find Meryl and Amy sitting in their light pink dresses under the Prophet's portrait, surrounded by a handful of my brothers and most of my sisters. "We're the luckiest people in the world," Meryl tells them. "God chose our spirit before we came to earth to be one of His elite."

"What about the outsiders?" one of them asks.

I clear my throat to get their attention.

Meryl puts up a finger, instructing me to wait. I roll my eyes as she lifts her chin with authority. "The Gentiles will be destroyed in the end times," she says and opens her copy of *Pronouncements of the Prophet*.

My brothers and sisters shake their heads.

I shift, suddenly uneasy. Destroyed? I know this is true, but now that I've met a few outsiders, I can't help but wonder if God created them only to destroy them.

Meryl reads aloud: "'A man must hold the priesthood and have three wives to enter the celestial kingdom. A woman must be married to a man who holds the priesthood and has at least three wives. Otherwise, that woman will be doomed to spend eternity in a lower level of heaven or in hell.'"

Amy places a finger on Meryl's book. "So that means Mother will go to the highest heaven?"

Meryl nods. "That's right. Father has three wives, so she will spend eternity as an angel of heaven with Mother Lenora and Mother Dee."

Amy's forehead furrows into a question. "So, if Father marries again, will his new wife go to the highest heaven, too?"

"That's exactly right," Meryl says with an approving smile.

I look at the portrait of the Prophet and wonder if he will assign Father another wife. Some men in our community have more than three. The Vulture has twelve, and the Prophet has somewhere around thirty wives, praying at home for his release from prison.

"So then, what about me?" Amy says as she sits upright on the carpet. "Will I go to the highest heaven, too?"

Meryl hesitates, and I wipe my hands across my skirt. No one's really sure whether the Prophet will assign Amy in marriage or not. Most girls are at least eighteen before they get married, and the only other girl who had Down syndrome died before her eighteenth birthday. Besides, some people say Amy won't be assigned because she's been cursed as punishment for Mother's progressive upbringing. If she's not married, Amy won't go to the celestial kingdom.

I swallow hard. "Of course you will," I say and enter the sunken living room.

Meryl closes her mouth and nods.

Amy's face relaxes.

I give her a teasing nudge. "But before you go up to heaven, Mother wants you to help me slice the bread, okay?" I take her by the hands and help pull her from the floor.

Meryl carefully closes her book. "Can I help?" She stands and places it on a table where Mother's piano used to be.

"Do whatever you want," I say and turn away, but not before seeing the hurt on Meryl's face.

I know I don't have any right to be mad at her. It's not her fault people gossip about Amy. And she *did* save my violin from the God Squad. But she's also the one giving Uncle Max a weekly report on me, and she's such a know-it-all. Tanner used to be the buffer between us, but with him gone, she constantly gets under my skin.

As we return to the kitchen, Mother comes up the stairs, looking flustered. She brushes the wisps of hair that have fallen from the hair-sprayed wave above her forehead. "That was your father." She turns to Mother Dee and Mother Lenora. "Uncle Max will be joining us for dinner tonight."

"Who else is coming?" Mother Dee asks as she opens the dish cabinet. "I don't think we have enough glasses for his whole family."

Mother shakes her head. "It's just him." She takes a deep breath, as if trying to calm herself. "Meryl, go tell your brothers and sisters. Make sure everyone's face is washed, and they're all wearing clean clothes."

Meryl quickly nods. "Yes, ma'am," she says and brushes past me like a whirlwind to gather the others.

Mother snaps her fingers. "Bread, you two."

Amy and I hurry over to the counter that holds the loaves. I pull a knife from the block, and the silver blade suddenly reminds me of Kel and the deer. The knife clatters against the countertop.

"Careful," Mother Lenora warns.

Bile rises up the back of my throat as I pass the knife to Amy. "You do it."

She picks up a loaf of wheat bread, whispering, "I don't like it when Uncle Max is here. He eats with his mouth open."

I swallow and nod with a whisper, "So gross."

Amy smiles as I place the slices in a basket and move it to the table. We repeat the same pattern a few times.

Father strides in as we're filling the final basket with white bread. "How are my girls?" he asks, looking happier than I've seen him in a long time.

"Good, Father," Amy and I say in unison.

The Vulture slips in behind him and makes eye contact. "Ladies," he says and then turns in the direction of the living room, like he's looking for someone else.

Father washes his hands in the kitchen sink. "Smells delicious."

Mother Lenora smiles wide from the compliment. "It's the meat that makes it smell so good."

Meat? Since the Prophet cut our rations, we rarely have the opportunity to eat meat anymore.

Mother Dee races between the tables, filling the glasses with water. Amy places butter on the tables.

My mouth waters. We haven't eaten meat in weeks.

Mother Lenora nods at Uncle Max. "We're obliged to you for sending it over."

"Oh, don't thank me," he says, his eyes still wandering the house. "Dirk insisted on sharing it with your family."

My heart stops as I choke on his name. "Dirk?"

"That's right." The Vulture's dark features twist into a crooked smile.

That's when I realize: the stew.

My stomach takes a final turn as my brothers and sisters file into the kitchen. I drop the last basket and rush the opposite direction, my feet pounding down the stairs before it's too late.

"Gentry," Mother calls. "Gentry, are you all right?"

I fall to my knees on the hard tile, hunch over the toilet, and dry heave. But there's nothing in my stomach to throw up. I had a tiny breakfast and couldn't eat lunch after survival class and now . . .

"What's gotten into you?" Mother says, running a cloth under the bathroom faucet. She places the cool rag against my neck.

"The stew," I mutter.

Mother's face turns to worry. "Oh no, Gentry. You're not sick, are you?"

I shake my head. "The deer."

"You're not making any sense," Mother says, and feels my forehead. "You do feel a little hot."

"Hannah, you've missed it," Father says, a laugh to his voice as he fills the doorway of the small bathroom.

Mother shakes her head. "I'm sorry, but Gentry doesn't feel well."

Father waves his hand in the air. "Oh, she'll be fine," he says, dismissing me. "You missed the good news." His smile widens. "The Prophet called."

"Thanks be—"

But Father interrupts her, "He had a revelation that Meryl is to be sealed in marriage."

My guts twist again.

Mother's hand covers her mouth before it slides down her neck. "But she's only fifteen, Conway."

"You haven't heard the best part: She's going to marry Max."

Suddenly, I can't breathe. I taste bile.

Father excitedly grabs Mother's shoulders. "Hannah, our daughter's going to marry the bishop of Watchful."

I turn and throw up.

9.

Meryl stands in front of a full-length mirror and sniffles again. Even under the yellowing fluorescent lights of Mother's basement sewing room, I can see my sister's eyes are red and puffy from crying into her pillow. I want to ask her if she's doing okay, but the Prophet teaches emotions belong to the devil and shouldn't be discussed.

That's probably why she refused to talk about it, even though it was just the three of us—Amy, Meryl, and me—in our room last night. After lights-out, I reached across the space between our beds and found her hand. Meryl squeezed until she finally cried herself to sleep.

Sitting here on the floor of Mother's sewing room, I know I'm supposed to be happy for my sister. After all, getting married is the highest honor for a girl in our church. It's what we live for, or at least what we're supposed to live for. But the

Prophet has proclaimed my most beautiful sister will be sealed for all time and eternity to Uncle Max, a man thirty years older than her and creepier than a bucket of rattlesnakes.

I don't feel very happy about it. I feel betrayed and disgusted and mostly sad for all of us. First, the Prophet took away my friend Channing. And then, Tanner. And now, Meryl.

Amy shadows Mother with a pincushion as she shapes and tucks the simple white fabric around Meryl's body, forming a wedding dress. With everything that's been happening, I miss music now more than ever.

While Mother and Amy tighten the back of the dress, I scoot on the floor, inch by inch, toward Mother's cutting table. I check over my shoulder to make sure they're not looking and pull my violin case from its hiding spot beneath the table.

With a breath, I open the case. My honey-colored instrument lies waiting for me in blue velvet. I press my lips together and silently glide my finger along the A string, longing to play.

"Grab that lace for me, will you?" Mother says, startling me. I knock my head against the bottom of the table and accidentally pluck the string. The note reverberates throughout the room, and I quickly mute it with the palm of my hand. My chest tightens.

Amy's eyes go wide behind her glasses.

The top of my head throbs. "S-sorry, I didn't mean to," I say as I check Meryl's reflection. But she doesn't even seem to notice what I've done.

"Another pin, please," Mother says to Amy. Mother moves around Meryl, ready to secure the next fold, acting as if nothing happened.

"But wait, what did you—" I fumble to close my case. "You said lace?"

"That one." She points to the trim she's pulled from her fabric closet.

Amy gives me a relieved smile as I hop up to retrieve the bolt of wide white lace from Mother's sewing chair.

Mother gestures to Meryl's front. "Try and overlay that across the top, will you?"

"Yes, ma'am," I say, wiping my sweaty fingers across my skirt before I hand Amy the scalloped edge. She takes it and we stretch the lace across Meryl's bodice, revealing the delicate floral pattern.

Mother looks at Meryl's reflection with an approving smile. "There. Do you like it?"

Amy pushes her glasses up her nose and enthusiastically nods. "It's so pretty."

Meryl's sullen face remains unchanged in the mirror. She shifts a little, her hip jutting to the side, as she seems to evaluate herself. Even with her puffy eyes and red nose, Meryl is still my most beautiful sister.

She sniffles and shrugs.

Mother's shoulders sink. "All right," she says, her disappointment obvious. Amy drops the edge of the lace as Mother nods to herself. "Keep heart. We'll find it. We haven't checked the scraps yet," she says, her voice suddenly too perky. "There might be a hidden treasure in them."

With new energy, Mother rifles through a pile of folded scrap fabrics, remnants from past dresses. I roll up the jilted lace and place it on her cutting table.

The phone rings.

"That darn phone," Mother Lenora's muffled voice huffs from the kitchen upstairs. Her footsteps thud across the floor as the phone rings again. "I'm going to rip it straight out of the wall if it keeps ringing like this."

Mother's expression tightens as she spies the clock on the wall. "Girls, give me a second," she says, dropping the scrap as she hurries from the sewing room and down the hallway toward the telephone. "I'll get it!" she shouts upstairs.

The phone rings again.

"It's about time," Mother Lenora replies, her voice a little louder. "Here I am trying to cook for the entire family, while you play dress-up with Meryl."

I edge to the doorway as Mother answers on the fourth ring. She turns toward the wall, as if trying to hide. She doesn't seem to notice me spying on her.

Mother cups her hand over the receiver to mute her voice. "Now's not a good time."

Who's she talking to? She turns away from me, and I take a small step into the hallway, craning my neck to hear.

"Call me back?" She pauses to listen. "No, Thursday's the wedding." Mother nods and whispers, "Okay, talk to you then."

Who could she be talking to? By now, Uncle Max has made sure the entire community of Watchful knows the exact date of the wedding.

"I love you, too," Mother whispers.

My heart stops. She never says that to Father.

"What's going on?" Amy asks as she sneaks up behind me.

My hand covers my racing heart.

"What?" Amy asks. "Is she talking to Tanner again?"

I spin around to face my sister; she slaps a hand over her mouth. *Tanner?* I grab her wrist, trying to pull her hand from her lips. "What did you say?"

Amy mumbles through her fingers. "Nothing."

Mother straightens her skirt as she nears. "All right, back to work, girls."

"Is it true?" I ask her. "Was that really him?"

She brushes past us, returning to the sewing room and acting as if she didn't hear me.

My mind races. "Where is he? Is he okay? Why didn't you let me talk to him?"

Mother gives me a look of warning, shutting me up, before she lowers her voice, "Let's discuss this later."

But I desperately want to find out how my brother's doing.

"Please," Mother says, her eyes begging as Mother Lenora's footsteps echo across the kitchen floor. She sternly points at the ceiling. "Later."

I press my lips together and nod, remembering the Prophet forbids anyone from associating with apostates. We could all get into trouble for merely saying my brother's name.

"Can I go upstairs now?" Meryl asks.

"Absolutely not," Mother barks, redirecting her focus. "The wedding is in a few days, and we have too much to do."

Meryl folds her arms over her chest. The fabric between her shoulders pulls and then rips a little.

Amy winces.

"Nobody's going to care what I'm wearing," Meryl says.

"I care," Amy whispers.

Mother shakes her head as she spins Meryl around to examine the tiny tear with her fingers. "Your future husband certainly will."

"Why?" Meryl shrinks from Mother's probing fingers. "I'm going to be his thirteenth wife. It's not like it's going to be *his* first wedding."

Mother's cheeks flush. "Meryl."

"Mother," Meryl responds with a sarcasm so sharp it slices the air between us. Our mother's eyes cut in my direction, as if she's making sure she hadn't misheard and it was really me who said it.

I shake my head as Meryl's hands land on her hips. "What are you looking at Gentry for?"

It's the first time I've ever heard Meryl act disrespectful to Mother. To anyone. If the circumstances weren't so horrible, I'd be cheering: My perfect sister isn't so perfect anymore.

But, as it is, I feel sorry for them both. They're so miserable. We all miss Tanner. Deep down, I don't think any of us, except Father, really want this wedding to take place.

Mother sighs, her palm against her stomach. "You must open your heart to what the Prophet has revealed for your life." It sounds like she's trying to convince herself as much as my sister. "This is the Prophet's calling and your mission."

"The Prophet's?" Meryl says with a dry laugh. "I think you mean *Father's.*"

My jaw drops.

"Bite your tongue," Mother snaps as she starts pacing the

room. "Your eternal salvation depends on this."

"Father used me," Meryl says, pressing her hand against her chest. "He traded me off as if I was nothing more than an old car part. Just so he could get Uncle Max off his back."

I suddenly feel off-balance. "What's she talking about?"

"Please don't fight," Amy says.

Meryl whips around to face me, her hair slipping from her braid in all directions. "You better watch your step. You could be next."

I've never seen her so undone. My insides twist.

"Enough!" Mother shouts, startling us all.

Amy covers her ears.

Mother slams her fist on the table. "You will *not* talk about your priesthood head in that manner."

"Why not?" Meryl retorts. "It's true."

My gaze darts between their angry faces. "What's true?" Although Meryl's the youngest girl I know to get married, I've heard stories of girls younger. But that was a long time ago, I think. I hope. "Mother?"

Mother takes a deep breath. "You're only thirteen. You're far too young to get married."

I manage a breath.

"What about me?" Meryl cries, her anger fading into desperation. "I'm too young, too, aren't I?"

Mother's eyes fall to the hem of her long skirt.

Meryl moves away from the mirror and snatches Mother's hands, commanding her attention. "I can't do this. Please, *please* talk to Father. I just need a few more years."

I nod as the rip on the back of her dress grows. Yes, please help her.

Mother shakes her head. "You belong to the Prophet, and he has revealed your path."

A whimper escapes Meryl's lips.

Amy's hands drop from her ears as Mother slides her fingers from Meryl's grasp. "Now, if I remember correctly, Mother Dee used a white satin ribbon on Gwen's blanket. I'm going upstairs to see if she has any left. And when I return, you will do best to remember who you are."

Her feet pound up the stairs; my heart sinks with each step. Mother has made her choice: the Prophet over her own daughter. Over her own son. Just as her faith requires.

"Why's she mad at me?" Amy wheezes, tears forming in her eyes.

"She's not," Meryl and I say in unison.

"She's mad at *me*," I say and approach Amy to give her a hug.

Meryl smears the tears from her cheeks and wraps her arms around both of us. "*And* me," she says.

The three of us hold one another for a few seconds when I

whisper, "How long has she been talking to Tanner?"

Meryl sniffles. "Pretty much since he left."

"Why didn't you tell me?"

Amy catches her breath. "I wanted to tell you since we don't keep secrets." From how she says it, I can tell it's been eating her up inside.

"Mother didn't want you to get your hopes up," Meryl adds. "She made us promise not to say anything."

I clench my jaw, disappointed they didn't tell me anyway. But at least now I know Tanner's alive.

After a few seconds, Amy turns to Meryl, her voice raspy. "Why don't you like your dress?"

Meryl takes a deep breath, encouraging Amy to do the same. I take one, too. We stand there for a second—forehead to forehead to forehead—and breathe. I wish I could freeze time. I miss Tanner so much, and as much as she can bug me, I don't want Meryl to leave, either. I nearly say so when she whispers, "I like the dress. I'm sorry."

I nod. "I'm sorry, too."

"Me too," Amy says, and Meryl and I laugh a little.

Meryl gives Amy an extra squeeze. "But you didn't do anything wrong, remember?"

Amy smiles. "But I probably will."

We laugh again.

"I bet Gentry beats you to it," Meryl says, playfully smacking my arm with the back of her hand.

"*Hey,*" I say, rubbing the place she hit and pretending to be offended. It's the first genuine smile I've seen on her face since she learned of the engagement. I don't want to ruin the moment, but what she said is still nagging me. "What did you mean when you said I could be next?"

The joy slides away from Meryl's face, and I immediately regret asking.

Meryl walks over to the cutting table and flips on the lamp to examine the lace under the light. She shrugs. "I guess I thought my age would protect me." She fingers the delicate flowers. "I honestly thought I'd be able to finish school before I got married."

I step toward her. "Who said you can't finish school?"

Meryl drops the edge of the lace and presses her hands together. "I'll be a wife. And soon, a mother. Uncle Max says there won't be any time for me to go to school."

My back stiffens. "But he has twelve other wives to do stuff around the house. Why can't he let you finish school?"

"I don't get to go to school, and I'm okay," Amy says, trying to console Meryl, but it makes me feel guilty all over again. When Mother brought Amy to start school with all the other kids her age, Uncle Max turned her away. In front of everybody.

He said she wasn't capable of learning. My hands clench from the memory. She cried for a whole week after that.

Meryl nods at Amy with a small smile. "Come now. You're more than okay."

Amy carefully touches the white fabric sleeves, pinned on Meryl's soon-to-be wedding dress. "What's wrong with being a wife and mother?"

"Nothing," Meryl says with a sigh. "I just didn't expect it to happen so soon, that's all."

I know I shouldn't question the Prophet's choice for her, but now Meryl has me wondering whether this match is truly the will of God or something else.

"He's so old," Meryl weakly says under her breath and then falls against me. I don't know what else to do, so I hold my sister. Tight.

Amy joins in, and over her shoulder, I spot my violin case on the floor. My breath catches as the puzzle pieces suddenly snap into place. "This is because of me, isn't it?"

Meryl slips from our embrace, denying it a little too quickly. "That's ridiculous."

"But if you hadn't stuck up for me about my violin, Uncle Max wouldn't have been coming over here so much, and maybe Father—"

Meryl grabs my hand, stopping my downward spiral. "It's

not your fault. I don't want you to think that *ever*."

"But it is my fault," I say, wrenching free of Meryl's grasp. "I have to do something."

Amy nods. "I wanna help, too."

"No," Meryl says, firm as she points between us. "You two will do nothing. Understand?" She's sounding a little more like her usual bossy self, but this time, her words ring hollow. She clears her throat and nods. "If this is what has been revealed to the Prophet, then Mother's right: We should not question." She touches Amy's cheek, reassuringly. "I just got a little nervous, that's all. All better now." Then, Meryl glances at herself in the mirror, as if seeing the new dress-in-progress for the first time.

She checks the rip in the back and lifts her chin. "Perfect obedience produces perfect faith and, thereby, perfect people." When Meryl repeats the Prophet's well-known phrase, Amy says it with her. They both look to me, expecting me to join them the third time around. But I can't. Not when, deep down, this all feels so wrong. I have to do something to stop the wedding. But what?

A scream from upstairs yanks me from my thoughts.

"Was that Mother Lenora?" Meryl asks.

We all run upstairs to find Mother Lenora hunched over in a kitchen chair, crying. "My baby, my baby," she says over and over.

A red-faced Buckley looms quietly over her, his black felt hat in hand.

We're a little winded from the stairs. Our chests heave as we look to ourselves and around the room for answers. Father's not here to give them.

Most of Mother Lenora's children stand around her, still. Kate looks pale by the window.

Finally, one of Mother Lenora's sons rushes in, followed by Mother Dee with Gwen strapped around her middle. Mother's on their heels, carrying a spool of white satin ribbon. "We're here. What happened?"

Kate cries softly into the sink. "It's Kel," she says, sounding heartbroken as she turns my direction. "He ran away."

10.

From Watchful's highest hill, I shiver against the dry November wind and hug my arms around my chest. The brittle white sage rustles around us. Next to me, Amy buzzes her lips and zips her jacket over her long dress.

"Should we look for Kel again?" Amy asks, her voice bobbing up and down as she tries to keep warm. She plunges her hands deep inside her pockets.

I nod, even though I know it's no use. Buckley told me, when Father stopped to gas his truck this morning, Kel jumped out and ran toward a rusted orange pickup. He sped off and disappeared before Father could even react.

Even though I know he's long gone, I couldn't stand to be in the house another second. Not with all the yelling and blame going around.

Buckley and his God Squad questioned each of us. Twice.

But the answer remains the same: We don't know anything. Kel's always been good with secrets. And in the last few hours, he's become one.

We're not supposed to talk about him anymore. He's an apostate now, and we're supposed to forget about him. I don't see how when I still haven't forgotten about Tanner.

The sun dips in the sky and saturates the clouds in fiery red and orange. The smell of piñon smoke wafts from the houses below and tickles my nose.

Amy sneezes. "See him?" she asks with a sniffle.

"Not yet," I answer as my gaze stretches beyond our wall that keeps the rest of the world out and to the purple-and-gray mountains in the distance. Kel is out there somewhere. And Tanner, too.

In only a few days, Meryl will be sealed to Uncle Max. Even though she's only moving to the other side of Watchful, somehow it feels like she's moving just as far away as Tanner and Kel. I wish there was something I could do to stop the wedding.

From out of nowhere, I hear the slip of gravel and spot Kate running uphill. Clouds of icy breath obscure her face. "There you are," she says when she reaches us. She hunches over, her hands on her knees as she catches her breath. "I've been looking all over for you."

The cold breeze blows the dark hair that's fallen from her

braid, and in the dimming sunlight, I can see the fresh bruise across her cheek.

Amy gasps as she seems to see it, too. "Did you fall?"

Kate stands straight and clenches her jaw.

I stiffen. "Who did that to you?"

"Buckley," she says with an exasperated sigh. "He just couldn't believe Kel's own twin didn't know anything about him running away."

"I'm sorry," I say and then hesitate for a second. If anyone would know something, it would be Kate. "*Did* you know about it?" I ask under my breath.

She takes a step backward. The wind kicks up, and she wraps her coat tight around her.

But I press onward anyway. "Did you know he was going to run away?"

Kate turns toward the sunset. By now, the color of the sky has deepened to a soft, hazy rose. The mountains look black against the fading light. "I guess I suspected. He's been questioning a lot of things lately," she admits and then shakes her head. "Don't tell anyone, but I think killing that deer was the breaking point."

"He killed a deer?" Suddenly, Amy's look of sympathy is replaced by a look of horror. "Why would he do that?"

"It wasn't his fault," I say, disgusted with Dirk all over again.

"Dirk made him do it yesterday in survival class."

A tear rolls down Amy's cheek. "Poor deer."

I rub circles on her back, trying to comfort her. "We won't say anything," I tell Kate.

Amy wipes her nose with her sleeve. "I won't, either."

"Thanks," Kate says and suddenly seems to remember something, jumping to attention. "Oh, I forgot. It's Meryl."

Goose bumps rush my arms. "What about her?"

She looks away again, like she's second-guessing herself.

"Tell me," I say. "Please?"

Kate sighs. "After all this stuff with Kel, Uncle Max moved the wedding to tonight."

"What?" I screech.

Amy shakes her head. "I don't understand."

"He's forbidden any of us from attending," Kate says, sounding annoyed.

"But we're her family," I say, desperate. "What about the preparations?"

"Her dress isn't finished yet," Amy adds.

"They're over," Kate says. "Father and Mother Hannah are heading to the meetinghouse with her now."

Before I can think, my feet take off. The cold wind stings my eyes as I run downhill, my shoes slip-sliding on the pebbles.

This can't be happening. It feels as if my family's being

ripped apart. Layer by layer, they're being torn away from me. I can't lose my half brother *and* my sister all in the same day. I just can't.

Darkness now inks the sky. My sleeve snags on a mesquite tree, stopping me for a second. A coyote howls in the distance. As I struggle to jerk free, clouds slither across the stars.

I consider leaving my jacket, but then manage to rip free of the branch, leaving a scrap of powder-blue cloth behind.

Cold air rushes through my sleeve, making it flutter, as I reach the bottom of the hill and dart to the right.

My shoes pound against the hard ground until I come to the dark stucco building with the flat roof. I yank open the heavy wooden door and, without stopping, run straight through the replica of the Prophet's prison cell.

Inside the large prayer room, the smell of disinfectant burns my nose. My eyes water. The Prophet's portrait is illuminated up front. The table with the phone we use to call the Prophet is beneath his portrait.

Uncle Max stands on the stage, facing the looming picture of the Prophet. Meryl is to Uncle Max's right in her light pink dress with the scalloped collar and white sash around her waist. His other wives stand on his left in accordance with the Law of Sarah, which gives them the privilege to accept Meryl into their home.

I pray I'm not too late. "Wait!" I yell, rushing up the aisle to the front of the room.

Meryl turns at the sound of my voice, hope flashing across her pale features. "Gentry?"

"What is *she* doing here?" Uncle Max crows.

Father jumps from his seat and turns, his face red with anger. "You shouldn't be here."

The Vulture's eyes narrow. "I specifically said none of your children could attend, Conway, and this is why. No respect."

As I approach the front, I can see the veins throbbing along the sides of Father's neck.

My feet stop a few inches from him. My heart's still running.

Mother rises from her seat and takes hold of Father's arm, as if to hold him back. Her eyes dart from my sweaty face to the hole in my sleeve. "What happened to your jacket?"

I almost laugh at how ridiculous her question is, but there's no time. Uncle Max has pushed the button on the table, calling in the God Squad. "I think I can fix this," I say.

Mrs. Whittier, our home economics teacher and the Vulture's first wife, scoffs. "Impertinent girl."

Uncle Max leaves center stage and flaps his arms with impatience. "Fix *what* exactly?"

I face his scowl. "I've just lost my brothers. Please. I can't lose my sister tonight, too."

"Give me one second, please," Meryl says as she moves away from Uncle Max, toward the stairs. She gives me a soft smile, speaking under her breath, "Gentry, I appreciate what you're trying to do."

Uncle Max follows her. "Who are you to barge in here like this and—"

"I'll give you my violin," I announce before I can change my mind. Meryl stops mid-step. "I-I know it's wrong to have it now," I admit. "I understand it's worldly. Please, if you'll just give us more time?"

"You're not thinking straight," Father scolds, a trace of hurt in his eyes. "I thought you wanted to keep your violin."

Mother releases his arm.

"I do, but not if it means Meryl has to get married now." I turn to Uncle Max. "Can you take it and just wait a little longer?"

Meryl descends the last steps. When she gets close, I can see Mother has woven her golden hair into an intricately braided crown upon her head. Meryl's fingers fiddle with the delicate sash around her waist. "You'd give up your violin for me?"

I nod.

Her eyes glisten with tears as she smiles.

"Sounds like someone has forgotten her place," a familiar voice booms through the speakers. My breath stutters as my eyes flash to the table again. The phone is in the docking station. "Have you not heard my revelation?" the voice says, growing louder.

My hands tremble. It's the living embodiment of God on earth: the Prophet.

Uncle Max's thin lips curl into a smile. "Indeed."

Meryl quickly wipes the tears from her cheeks.

I should have known. Uncle Max performs weddings in our community of Watchful. But who can perform the ceremony for him? Only the Prophet.

All of a sudden, the God Squad barges into the prayer room. Meryl takes hold of my elbow and swings me behind her. My heart races as Buckley leads the charge, his face redder than ever. Five goons follow, their straw hats covering their eyes.

"The Prophet speaks," the Vulture caws and holds out his long hand to stop them, mid-aisle.

The God Squad comes to an abrupt halt. "Thanks be to God," everyone in the room mutters. Everyone, but me.

"Who is it that defies me?" the Prophet asks.

I knead my hands in the tense silence until Uncle Max answers, "Gentry. Forrester."

My knees go slack, but Meryl manages to keep me upright.

"Ahh, I see," the Prophet continues.

Mother fans her face with her hand.

"Gentry, you must live faithfully," the Prophet says.

My cheeks flush hot. Father's shoulders sink. I wish I could shrivel and hide under one of the chairs.

"For marriage is God's will, spoken through the Prophet. In marriage, men become gods and women heavenly mothers. The husband holds the keys to a woman's blessings, and the Prophet holds the keys to the husband's." I nod along, knowing all this already, but the Prophet continues, "Without a husband, a woman is nothing. You should know by now that your sister's eternal salvation depends upon marriage to a priesthood man. As does yours. You do know that, right?"

Everyone turns, awaiting my answer. Even Meryl.

Yes, I know all this. But what if I want more for Meryl? For me? What if, deep down, I dare to want to be a wife and a mother, but with a future *I* choose?

"If your sister does not fulfill my revelation," the Prophet adds, "she will be stuck between worlds, alone forever. Is that what you want for her?"

Meryl nudges me, her eyes willing me to get out of my head and answer the Prophet.

Of course I don't want my sister to be alone forever. But I feel so torn. I know what's right, so why doesn't it *feel* right? Why does forever have to start right now for her?

The longer I stall, the more I can sense everyone's judgment spinning around me and trapping me like a spider's web. Even the Prophet's portrait is looking down on me. "N-no," I say, trying to talk past the tightness in my throat.

"Speak up," the Vulture squawks.

I open my mouth, but the Prophet interrupts, "If you turn away from my revelations, you will certainly be destroyed."

Meryl snatches my hand, her eyes filled with a new urgency. "It's time for you to go home now."

"But—"

She squeezes harder. "Thank you for your kindness," she says, sounding like a pre-programmed robot. "I will fulfill my duty. It is the only way. This marriage is what the Prophet has revealed for my life."

I shake my head. What's she doing?

"Go on home," she says resolutely, giving me a stiff hug before returning to the stage.

"Finally," Uncle Max says, pointing at the door. "Show her out."

Two of the God Squad approach. One of them takes me by the arm, but I twist free. "I'm going," I say, embarrassed and confused. I march to the rear of the prayer room.

"Wait," the Prophet's voice booms through the speakers. "Gentry should hear this."

"Stop her," the Vulture demands, but I've already stopped at the back of the room. I shiver as I turn toward the Prophet's portrait.

"Sometimes, an apple is beautiful," the Prophet says, his voice calm. "It can seem flawless even until you turn it around and see a scar—an imperfection, if you will."

My knees quiver.

"As God's chosen, we must throw out the bad apple before it rots the rest of the barrel."

My whole body's shaking. He's going to kick me out. He's going to kick me out with nowhere to go. No money. No shelter. No food. Nothing. Why didn't I pay more attention in survival class?

The Prophet clears his throat. "Your father has lost control over his family."

Meryl suddenly looks worried.

"I've lost confidence in him," the Prophet declares.

Father drops into the seat next to Mother. Like he's been pushed.

"Conway, are you still there?"

Father wipes his forehead with his handkerchief. "I'm here," he says after a second, his voice low.

There's a pop through the speakers. "Then rise," the Prophet says with conviction.

With a hand on the back of his chair, Father slowly gets to his feet. He shoves his handkerchief inside his pocket and looks at the portrait of the Prophet.

"He's standing," Uncle Max confirms.

"Very well," the Prophet says. "This wedding will move forward as planned."

The Vulture gives a smug nod.

"But first, I have received a holy revelation."

"Thanks be to God," the Vulture and some of his wives mutter in unison.

A lump lands in my throat. Father hunches forward, as if he's getting ready for a blow.

"Conway Forrester, you are no longer worthy to hold the priesthood."

Meryl covers her mouth. My throat tightens around the growing lump.

Father staggers, not ready. "But why?" he asks. "What have I done?"

I reach for the nearest chair, trying my best to keep from falling over.

"Do you question the will of the Prophet?"

"No," Father says immediately. "I'm loyal. I have always been loyal to you."

I nod. It's true. He's always been loyal.

The God Squad approaches him anyway.

The Prophet's breath flows through the speakers. "Your failure to reach perfection prevents the rest of our community from being lifted into heaven. For years, you have allowed an evil to seep into the foundation of your home."

Father's jaw trembles.

"You do not discipline your children as they should be disciplined. You have allowed worldly music."

Mother bites her knuckle.

"You have raised sons of perdition. And now, this daughter of yours thinks she's worthy of addressing the bishop of Watchful."

I swallow the lump.

The speakers pop again. "A darkness has settled over your household, Conway, and I intend to vanquish it once and for all," the Prophet says. "You must leave Watchful immediately and repent from afar."

My heart's racing. Mother clutches her chest. Meryl does the same.

"You will continue to tithe to the church and write a letter of confession. In time, if I deem it appropriate, I *might* allow you to return."

"And my family?" Father asks, his voice shaking as the God Squad takes hold of both of his arms.

I hold my breath and glance at the Prophet's portrait, awaiting his answer.

"They are no longer your family."

11.

I'm still staring at the Prophet's portrait at the front of the prayer room when I gasp. Father can't lose the priesthood.

Flanked by a pair of God Squad goons, Father wordlessly stumbles in place.

A sadness creases Mother's forehead, but she doesn't say anything. She doesn't move.

Uncle Max flaps at the God Squad. "Get him out of this holy place, so we may proceed with the wedding."

My heart thuds against my ribs. This isn't happening. Why would the Prophet take the priesthood away from my father?

"Father?" I ask, looking for some kind of explanation. But he stares straight ahead at the Prophet's portrait.

"It is done," the Prophet pronounces.

Meryl bites her lip. The Vulture's wives look stunned.

Then, footsteps sound through the speakers. "Time's up.

Off the phone," a man orders. It's the voice of an outsider.

"Await my call in the mor—" the Prophet says quickly and there's a click. Like he's hung up the phone. Or someone's hung it up for him.

Meryl hurries off the stage to join Mother. They embrace. There will be no wedding tonight.

The Vulture's face puckers in annoyance. "You heard the Prophet," he snaps. "Get him out of here."

The God Squad drags Father through the prayer room door and into the fake prison cell. He shouts over his shoulder, "Hannah, there's been some kind of mistake! I'll fix this."

Mother buries her face in her hands.

"Gentry!" Father shouts as the God Squad pulls him outside.

"Wait," I call after them, pushing through the meetinghouse door, but they don't stop. I hurry to catch them.

"We'll work this all out," Father says to me as the men hustle him toward the concrete wall. "You'll see. Everything will turn out fine."

When we reach the entrance to Watchful, the gears hum. The gate swings outward as one of the God Squad pushes Father outside the compound. Both of them aim their rifles at him.

My pulse races.

"You shall repent from afar," one of the goons orders.

Before I can think, I run past the gate and throw my arms around Father's waist. "I'm sorry, I didn't mean to. This is all my fault."

To my surprise, Father wraps his arms around me and holds me tight. I can't remember him ever holding me like this. It feels so good; I start crying.

"Keep your violin," he says under his breath. "Okay? Do it for me."

My tears wet his shirt. "Father, it doesn't matter now. You can't leave us."

He strokes the hair on top of my head and whispers, "You played beautifully at the festival. I knew you would, and you did. Keep your violin and think of me, okay?"

I nod against his chest.

"Promise?" he asks.

I nod again.

A hand grasps my jacket and yanks me backward. Before I can break free, the gate closes with a clang, separating me from Father and widening the gap between us.

***

By the following morning, our entire family has heard the horrible news, and we're all wondering what's going to happen next. Buckley has ordered us to gather in the living room, where everyone is strangely quiet.

My mothers sit in their usual places on the sofas. Baby Bill coos in Mother's arms; Meryl places a pacifier in his mouth. Gwen sleeps in the sling around Mother Dee, and Mother Lenora holds two of her sons in her lap. The rest of my brothers and sisters take their places on the carpet in front of the portrait of the Prophet.

Instead of sitting with Mother Lenora's children, Kate nestles in on one side of me. The bruise across her cheek has darkened from green to purple. Amy sits on my other side.

When we are all in place, Buckley escorts Uncle Max to Father's chair. I shift uncomfortably as the Vulture places a white cloth on the seat before lowering himself to the edge with his polished shoes flat on the floor.

He clears his long, bumpy throat. "I deliver a message from the Prophet."

"Thanks be to God," we all chime softly.

The Vulture's beady eyes narrow. "Conway Forrester has been deemed unworthy of the priesthood."

Amy sniffles. I put my arm around her. Uncle Max won't be happy if she starts crying. We must keep sweet.

"But why?" Kate asks, surprising me, asking the question we all want to ask, but are too afraid. Some of my brothers and sisters nod. "Yes, why?"

Uncle Max gives my half sister a cutting look. "Rebellious children are proof your father lost the spirit of God."

From out of nowhere, Mother Lenora rips Kate up by the wrist. She cries in pain.

The Vulture's lips twist into a smile.

Mother Lenora drags Kate through the seated children and into the kitchen, out of sight. We all sit in shock as we listen. "You." *Slap*. "Will." *Slap*. "Keep sweet." *Slap. Slap.*

After a second, Kate suddenly reappears, as if she's been shoved from behind. Red handprints cover her face and neck. She clutches her wrist. Tears fill her eyes, but she doesn't dare make a sound as she takes her place with the rest of Mother Lenora's children.

Mother Lenora adjusts her dress over her round waist as she enters the living room. She returns to the sofa as if nothing happened, pulling one of her trembling sons onto her lap.

"As I was saying," the Vulture croons with satisfaction, "the Prophet has determined each of his wives shall be reassigned in the following manner: Lenora, you and your children will live with Buckley and his family."

Mother Lenora's eyes flick to Buckley. He smiles, still standing behind the Vulture. Her eyes fall to the floor. "Thank you," she whispers.

"Dee," Uncle Max calls, and she looks up with hope. "Once Meryl has been sealed to me, you and your infant daughter will come to live with us."

Mother Dee swallows hard as some of the older kids gasp and mumble, realizing what this means. Because Meryl will be one of the Vulture's wives, and Mother Dee no longer has a husband, Meryl will rank higher in the family than Mother Dee. "Thank you," she says.

My shoulders relax a bit. At least this means we can stay in our own home with Mother. That way, Father knows exactly where to find us.

"As for Hannah," he says.

Mother bobs Baby Bill up and down in her arms, while Meryl clutches the edge of the sofa.

"You and your children have been reassigned to the bishop."

I glance at the Prophet's portrait and silently thank him. I don't like the idea of being assigned to the Vulture, but at least this way I can still see Meryl.

Meryl smiles at me and then hugs Mother. Amy and I jump up to join them and embrace them from behind the sofa.

"I think there may be a misunderstanding," the Vulture says.

Mother and Meryl separate as Uncle Max leans back in Father's chair and tents his long, bony fingers. "The Prophet has assigned you and your children to our brother."

My heart stops. My gaze flicks to the portrait again. He's sending us to his other brother: the bishop of Waiting.

"In Canada?" Meryl asks, her voice a whisper.

Uncle Max nods with a smile. "Over two thousand miles away."

12.

It's all my fault we're being sent away. Why'd I have to barge in on Meryl's wedding? Why'd I have to keep my violin? Why'd I have to go to the festival? I know I'm supposed to keep sweet. I know it. So why do I keep messing up?

Reassigned to three different men, my family has been blown apart. It feels as if the government has dropped a giant bomb in the center of our house. Only it's not the government. It's the Prophet.

"I don't see why we can't stay here," I say, eyeing Mother's open trunk on her bedroom floor. It's stuffed with clothes and blankets and things for Baby Bill.

Mother pulls a hairpin from between her teeth. "Obedience is the key to our salvation," she says as she fastens one of Meryl's braids into place.

I shift on the edge of Mother's bed. "But Father will be home soon. You heard the Prophet: When Father writes his letter of confession, he will return home. Why should we go over two thousand miles away only to turn around and come right back?"

Mother twists another braid through the first. "Gentry, I can't talk about this right now. Why don't you put it on a shelf and pray about it?"

I roll my eyes. What good will it do to put it on a shelf here in New Mexico when I'm going all the way to Canada?

"Perfect," Mother says with a satisfied grin. She holds up the wave above Meryl's forehead and sprays my sister's hair for an extra-long time, leaving her in a massive cloud of hairspray. "All finished."

I cough from the sticky mist.

Meryl lightly touches the back of her lacquered head and stands to unsnap the robe over her pink dress, the one with the scalloped collar and sash. She lays Mother's robe across the chair, offering a polite smile. "Thank you, Mother."

"I always knew you'd make a beautiful bride," Mother says, fiddling with the fraying cuff on her sleeve. "I only wish I could've finished your wedding dress."

Meryl straightens her skirt and nods. "This one is fine."

"Of course," Mother says, her voice cracking. "Of course

it is." She points to the hallway. "I think I'm going to go and help Amy pack."

"She's already packed," I remind her, but Mother rushes from the room anyway. I let out a sigh and look to Meryl. "I don't understand why Uncle Max won't let us at least stay for the wedding before we leave."

Meryl laughs a little. "I'm guessing he doesn't want another *interruption*."

"It's not funny," I say, pressing my palms flat against Mother's floral comforter. "Can't you see I've really messed things up this time?"

"Come on, it's a little funny." Meryl sits next to me on the edge of the bed, and I fall into her a bit. The smell of hairspray clings to her. She nudges me. "This started long before you ever decided to interrupt a wedding. It started before any of us were even born."

"What do you mean?" I ask.

Meryl's eyes check the hallway before she leans in, whispering, "Did you know Father ran away once?"

I remember the story Father told Tanner and me on the bridge over the Rio Grande Gorge. How he thought he wanted to leave the community when he was younger. I nod. "I think so."

"Do you know why Father left?"

I shake my head. I don't remember him mentioning why.

My sister folds her hands in her lap. "He left when the Prophet said it was time for him to take a second wife."

My eyebrows scrunch together. "But his second wife is Mother."

Meryl nods.

"So why did he want to run away?"

Meryl glances the direction of the hallway once more. Still no one there. "He had only been married to Mother Lenora for a year or so. He was so in love with her, he didn't want to marry anyone else."

"In love with Mother Lenora?" I ask, shock underlining my words.

My sister shushes me.

I swallow hard, realizing what she's saying. If he hadn't married Mother, none of us would even be here. "So why did he marry again?"

"Grandfather reminded him it was the way of God. That it was his duty to have multiple wives and children with those wives if he wanted to do right by God in this life and grant his family salvation in the next." Meryl sighs. "Father understood he was being selfish and returned to the community. He married Mother the next day."

"But he didn't love her," I say.

"Just like I don't love Uncle Max," my sister says matter-of-factly. "And like our parents, I'll fulfill my earthly mission."

Sounds more like a punishment to me.

"I don't want to end up like Tanner. I *want* to be able to see my family." She shudders. "And I can't stand the thought of being alone for all eternity."

I nod, understanding. Nobody wants to be alone, especially in the afterlife. Because that means forever.

Meryl squeezes my hand. "Promise me you'll stay strong."

"But they don't want me to be strong, remember?" They want me to keep sweet.

"You're right," she says and then holds up three fingers, the way she sometimes does when she's teaching my brothers and sisters something important. "Think of a swing set. Most people like to sit in the swing and get pushed, right?"

I nod, not sure where she's going with this.

One of her fingers goes down. "Then, there are the others who like to do the pushing." Another one down. "And then, there's an even smaller number who like to swing themselves. They control the height and the speed. They're also the only ones who know what it feels like to jump from the swing and fly." She smiles as her hand leaps through the air.

I look into her big blue eyes. "So which one am I?"

She pats my leg.

"The last one?"

Her smile brightens.

All these years, I've done my best to stay away from my big sister. I couldn't understand her; I thought she couldn't understand me. Suddenly it seems as if Meryl knows me better than I even know myself. She's my most beautiful sister, but now I see there's so much more to her than that.

The doorbell rings.

"Don't forget your violin." She jumps from the bed. "Now hurry. Your ride is here."

Reminded of my promise to Father, I rush downstairs and through the living room, past the portrait of the Prophet, and into the kitchen. Except for us, the house is quiet and empty. The doorbell rings again. I hurry to the basement and to Mother's sewing room before pulling back the scraps of fabric that hide my violin case.

With my case in hand, I rush upstairs to our room as Mother answers the door. I throw open my trunk and hide my violin at the bottom, beneath my sacred underwear. I slam the lid closed and latch it.

"There are two trunks in here," Mother says as she approaches our room.

When I look up, I spot the scars on his hand before I see his rigid face in my doorway. My stomach drops.

It's Dirk.

***

The van bounces in a rut, waking me as Dirk turns off the main road and drives through a narrow break in the trees. Snow crunches beneath our tires. I wipe the sleep from my eyes and peer out the window into the endless darkness.

We've been in the van for over two days now, stopping only a few times along the way. I've barely moved from my seat in the back, the farthest I could get from Dirk. Amy sleeps on my shoulder, snoring softly. Mother looks back at me with an exhausted smile, keeping a hand on Baby Bill, who's asleep in his car seat. "Almost there," she whispers.

Within a few minutes, there's a beacon of light up ahead. It shines brightly on a chain-link fence and a guard, dressed in all black. His eyes are barely visible beneath a black hat and the scarf that wraps around the bottom half of his face. I nudge Amy awake and look through the windows on both sides of the van.

"Where are we?" she asks.

"Waiting," Dirk answers, making me shiver.

When we approach the gate of our sister community, he nods to the guard. Snow dusts the entire fence line that seems to go on for miles and miles in both directions. The chain link rattles from the guard's touch, making some of the snow sail off and sparkle beneath the light before it falls to the covered ground.

As we move beyond the fence, I see nothing but snow ahead and a web of leafless trees on either side. I've been told about the same number of people live in Waiting as in Watchful, but I guess the houses are more spread out, because I can't see any of them now.

The van's engine moans as we move uphill. Amy leans toward me, whispering, "This would be a good place to sled."

I manage a smile and nod, doubting I'll ever sled again. I promised myself I'll try harder this time. I'll keep sweet. The less trouble I cause, the more likely the Prophet will realize that Father is good for us. And the sooner Father returns home, the sooner we can, too.

When we reach the top of the hill, the van rolls to a stop. The bishop of Waiting has eighteen wives and around fifty children still living at home, but I didn't realize his house would be this big.

"Wow," Amy says, her mouth falling open when she sees the massive cabin.

Built with dark brown logs, the structure is three stories high with snow covering the A-line roof that tops each sprawling wing of the house.

It's the middle of the night, but every window is illuminated by a soft yellow glow. My stomach flip-flops. They're waiting up for us.

The painted front door flies open and out steps a burly, round-faced man with gray hair. Dirk cuts the engine and jumps from the van. He shakes the man's hand.

With the door open to the van, it doesn't take long for the heat to escape. But we remain seated.

"Is that Uncle Hyram?" Amy whispers as the man signals for us to come inside.

I shrug, unsure.

"Now, girls," Mother says as she pulls Baby Bill from his seat. His head falls sleepily against her shoulder as she opens the door. "Remember your manners."

The gray-haired man greets Mother as Amy and I grab our coats. Outside, my shoes slip on the packed snow, but I manage to stay upright.

"Careful there," a man says from the shadows a few feet away. It takes me a second to find him, because he's dressed in all black, head to toe. There's a gun strapped to his side. I quickly turn away. God Squad.

Cold air stings my skin as I hurry around the van and help Amy step outside.

"Welcome, ladies," the pudgy, gray-haired man says from the doorway of the cabin.

I steal a glance at the guard and quickly turn away when I realize he's still watching us.

"Are you Uncle Hyram?" Amy asks.

"Amy," Mother scolds. "You know who this is."

Uncle Hyram gives a hearty laugh, his hands against his large stomach. "That's quite all right. It's been a while since I've been down to Watchful."

Mother's face holds a tense smile.

I clear my throat. "Thank you for allowing us to stay with you, sir."

Uncle Hyram nods, the folds of his neck scrunching against his stiff collar. "You're quite welcome, young lady." Then he gestures us into the house. "You all must be exhausted. Please come in from the cold."

We follow him inside and Mother mouths tenderly to me, *Thank you.*

I smile back at her. That's right. I'm going to show everyone I can keep sweet.

Uncle Hyram leads us into a large living area with a stone fireplace. The air smells stale, like the house hasn't been aired out since summer. The Prophet's life-size portrait hangs above the roaring fire. The warmth seeps into my skin as I remove my coat.

"Dirk," Uncle Hyram says, "tell your aunts you've arrived."

With a nod, Dirk leaves the room, and my shoulders begin to relax. My neck cracks as I turn my head. I hadn't realized how tense I'd been with him around.

Uncle Hyram sits on an easy chair, much like Father's. "Everyone should be here in a minute."

"Can we look at the pictures?" Amy asks, pointing to a long wall of photos.

Uncle Hyram nods. "Please do."

Amy and I near a series of wedding photographs of Uncle Hyram and each of his wives, with him getting progressively older and his wives seeming to get progressively younger in each picture. As we move around the room, there's a series of built-in shelves. I wander over to the photos, which appear to be each family grouping since there are eighteen frames total with a picture of Uncle Hyram, one of his wives and their children in each.

In the center of the shelves, there's an older photograph, but I recognize Uncle Max immediately. Uncle Hyram is in it, too. They're both younger and stand on either side of the Prophet. It's the three brothers who lead our church.

"That was taken right before the outsiders got him," Uncle Hyram says over my shoulder and points to the Prophet. "At the last Pioneer Day celebration." He turns to Mother. "Do you remember that fine day?"

Mother covers a yawn and nods. "Like it was yesterday."

"You made it," a tiny woman says as she glides into the living room with a broad smile. Lines of children file in behind her, pressed and clean. "I'm Pearline. Welcome to Waiting."

I glance at the first wedding portrait on the wall behind her, where the top of the wife's head comes to Uncle Hyram's stomach. This must be his first wife. Only now, she has a few more wrinkles, and her hair has streaks of white.

With Baby Bill in her arms, Mother nods her thanks and joins us against the shelves in order to get away from the traffic of incoming wives and children.

They enter the room and line up, one by one, eighteen clusters at a time. All of the girls wear the same blank expression with the same perfect wave of hair above their foreheads.

As the final child gets carried in, Dirk returns to stand by his uncle. My shoulders bump against the wall of shelves. The living room suddenly feels hot and cramped.

"She only has three children?" a girl asks. The kids around her shush her.

My heart sinks. No, there aren't three of us. There's over

twenty of us, and I want to go home.

"What's wrong with that one?" one of the boys says, pointing at Amy as she yawns. My hands clench as he's elbowed. Thankfully, Amy seems too tired to have noticed what he said.

The sheer number of them is overwhelming. I really hope we don't have to stay long.

"This is my family," Uncle Hyram says, like he's showing them off. Which he probably is since the more wives and children he has, the better off he'll be in the hereafter. "Pearline has prepared your rooms."

"You're too kind," Mother and I say. Like we're supposed to do.

Pearline smiles. "The boys will get your things from the van. Follow me."

We do as we're told and trail her, passing by the front door before we move into a long, narrow hallway. A series of hooks line the wall. "You can hang your coats here," she says and we place them on the bare hooks. "You're lucky you're on my floor," Pearline continues when we reach the steep staircase. "It's a little quieter."

"That's wonderful," Mother says, obviously exhausted and ready to get some sleep. My legs are like weights as I drag them to the third floor. Boys shove our backs and pass us, running down the hallway.

"Boys," Pearline scolds, but they laugh as they run into one of the rooms and slam the door.

"You have boys and girls on the same floor?" Mother asks, shock coloring her voice.

Pearline stops in the middle of the hallway and turns, the smile gone from her face. Even though she's shorter than all of us, it suddenly feels as if she's looking down on Mother. "When you have this many children, Hannah, you don't get the luxury of separating them."

Mother clears her throat and nods. "Yes, of course. Please forgive me."

The politeness returns to Pearline's face. "All right then. Your room is this way."

Mother lowers her head and follows, trailed by Amy and me. Pearline keeps talking about schedules for the laundry and cooking, and I soon tune her out. I glance into the rooms as we pass. There are at least four beds in each. By the fifth or sixth room, I hear, "Psst." I stop and hear it again. "Psst, psst."

A pair of boys runs past me and knocks into my shoulder without stopping. I rub my arm and look backward.

"Come here," a girl's voice whispers. "I want to talk to you."

I back up until I see her. She has light-blond hair, almost white. She smiles. "Come here."

I smile, grateful to meet someone friendly and about my

age. But when I get to the door, she slams it in my face. Cruel laughter erupts inside the room.

I knead my lips and turn to find Mother and Amy. But they're already gone. Most of the doors are closed. Where did they go?

"They're in there," a boy says, peeking out of his room.

I hesitate and then point to a closed door. "Here?"

He nods.

I open the door, and suddenly someone shoves my back, pushing me inside. The door slams behind me, trapping me in the dark. I hear a click. Giggles fade down the hallway. My fingers find the doorknob, but it's no use. It's locked. Familiar panic seizes me. My hand slaps against the door. I try the door-knob again and push and pull. "Help." My heart races. "Help me! Please." My fingernails scrape the wood.

In an instant, the door flies open and I fall to the hall floor, landing next to a pair of boy's shoes.

"Are you all right?" he asks.

I brush the tears from my cheeks and quickly look up.

He's a little taller now, but his dark hair flops across his forehead like it always has.

It can't be him. Meryl said he's supposed to be in hiding with his family. "Channing?"

13.

Awakened by nightmares of slamming doors, tight spaces, and darkness, I can't really sleep. I carefully edge away from Amy and toss the blanket from my legs, letting my eyes adjust to the unfamiliar room. A slant of pale moonlight streams through the window and touches the foot of Mother's bed. I check again. Still no trunk.

I have to get my violin. But where is it?

The house is quiet. I slip on my boots and tiptoe across the carpet in yesterday's clothes before moving into the long hallway. I hold my breath as I pass a series of closed doors, snores issuing from some of the bedrooms.

Moonlight from a small overhead window washes the stairway with a bluish glow. I creep down the steep stairs, careful to hold on to the log walls so I don't trip. When I reach the first floor, I retrace my steps from the night before, hoping the boys left my trunk by the front door. But it's not there.

I clench and unclench my fists and move into the living room with all the pictures on the wall. The fire is down to embers and ashes. The family groupings stare at me. Even though it's mostly dark, I can still see the pale flesh of the Prophet. I shiver and search the floor. Still, no trunk.

Out of nowhere, a flash of movement catches my eye. I gasp as a darkened figure comes closer. And then turns on a small lamp.

"What are you doing down here?" Channing whispers.

I manage to breathe, slowing my heart. Until I see what he's carrying. "What are you doing with that?"

He clasps my violin case to his chest. "Hiding it."

"You went through my trunk?" I ask, my voice beginning to rise with anger.

Channing covers his mouth with a finger, shushing me. "There was a raid a while back," he whispers. "The God Squad took anything that had to do with music and burned it."

My heart sinks. "We had that in Watchful, too." And then my cheeks heat all over again. "You went through my trunk?"

"The God Squad will search it in a few hours anyway. You got here so late, I didn't have time to tell you last night. I was going to hide it and tell you later."

"Still," I say, grateful to him but also suddenly embarrassed, realizing he touched my sacred underwear.

"You can come with me if you want," he says, gesturing to the front door. "But we have to go now. People will be getting up soon."

I nod, and he smiles before turning off the lamp.

"Let me grab my coat," I say, and rush to yank it off the hook and then join him at the front door.

The chill outside is immediate. My breath forms a cloud in front of my face as I look left and right. "Where's the guard?" I ask.

Channing shakes his head. "He doesn't come back until after sunup. The God Squad almost always stays along the fence at night."

We walk away from the house, the snow crunching beneath our boots.

"I can take that," I say, pointing to my violin case.

He stops for a second and holds his arm out straight. I reach for the handle and his hand accidentally brushes against mine. "Uh, sorry," he says, awkwardly shoving his hand inside his pocket as if he's cold, even though I can feel the warmth of his hand on the handle. My cheeks flush a little.

"This way," he says, and keeps moving toward a grove of tall bare trees. Inside the thicket, pockets of moonlight make the snow glow at our feet. The gray bark on the trees is peeling all around us. "Where are we going?"

Channing steps over a fallen branch. "The barn's on the other side of the river."

I step over the branch, too. "We're going to hide my violin in a barn?"

He stops, one eyebrow raised. "You've got a better idea?"

I press my lips together and shake my head.

Channing turns and resumes walking. "I'm usually the only one who goes in there. I feed and water the animals. Milk the cows."

"Aren't you worried you'll get into trouble for helping me?"

Channing releases a dry laugh. "I'm already in trouble. I thought you knew the Prophet sent me here for reform."

I shake my head, remembering how Channing was at school one day and then vanished the next without saying good-bye. When I asked Mother about it, she said the Prophet sent his family to pray for us in the mountains. It didn't make much sense at the time, but I kept sweet and didn't press. "What happened?"

"You mean why did I get sent here?"

I nod as we continue walking, the snow collapsing beneath our boots.

"You remember how I was getting sent to Uncle Max's office a lot before I left?"

"I remember the bruises," I say and then shrink inside my coat, knowing we're not supposed to talk about those things.

A thin branch blocks our path at eye level. Channing stops for a second and grabs hold, snapping it off in one motion. "Things weren't making as much sense as they used to." He starts tapping the trees' trunks with the broken-off branch as we pass them.

"Like what?" I ask.

"Like how can we be the only ones to have all the answers? And why would God create the outsiders just so He can destroy them?"

I clutch the handle on my case tighter, knowing exactly what he means. I used to feel special that God chose me—*me* of all people—to be saved. But after everything that's happened these last few months with my family, and after meeting outsiders who were nothing like I'd been taught, it's becoming harder and harder to believe everything I'm told.

"Uncle Max didn't like it much, so he sent me here for reform at the same time he threw out my dad and sent the rest of my family into hiding." Channing stops tapping the trees and starts dragging the stick through the snow, leaving a squiggly line between our footprints. "The idea is to work me so hard, I can't find any time to get into trouble."

I lift my violin case. "Looks like you're still finding time."

Channing chuckles to himself. "Yeah, I guess."

"So where's the rest of your family?"

He shrugs. "Don't know. I think my mother and brothers and sisters are somewhere in the mountains of Colorado." He shakes his head. "Uncle Hyram says if I keep up the good work, I'll get to see them again real soon."

"That's great," I say.

"Yeah," Channing agrees. He stops; his eyes go wide. He quickly turns his head. I hear it, too: the crunch of footsteps quickly approaching.

"God Squad," Channing whispers, urging me to duck behind a tree. My pulse throbs inside my ears. Channing raises his stick.

And then I see her blond hair in the moonlight. "Amy?" I say, lowering my violin case to the snow. I run to my sister.

"Are we exploring?" she asks with a sense of adventure in her voice.

I nod. "Something like that," I say and zip her coat. "How'd you find us?"

She points at the snow, her breath fogging in front of her face. "Footprints, silly."

I smile. "You're the smartest person I know."

"Don't you forget it," she says.

"Channing's showing me a place to hide my violin," I say, thumbing toward him. "It's super secret. You want to come?"

She smiles as I tug her toward Channing.

When we reach him, he drops the stick he's still holding.

"You remember Amy, don't you?" I say.

Channing nods. "What are you doing up so early?"

Amy juts out her jaw. "I'm not up any earlier than you."

I grin. "She's got a point, you know?"

He looks a little surprised, like he's never had two girls challenge him. Then he shrugs. "Let's keep moving then."

I retrieve my violin case from the snow and follow them through the grove. "These look like good climbing trees," Amy says, pointing to the branches overhead.

"They all look like good climbing trees to you," I tease.

"That's true," she says as we exit the thicket and reach a wooden bridge.

Channing cautiously steps onto the bridge. "Careful, it's icy," he warns.

Amy is right behind him, holding out her arms as she keeps her balance. I'm behind her when she squeals, "Gentry, look!"

From the corner of my eye, I see a streak of white hopping along the frozen river.

"Wow, even I have trouble spotting those," Channing says to Amy. "You must have really good eyes."

Amy pushes up her glasses with a nod.

Channing lifts a finger. "Do you know what *kind* of rabbit it is?" The rabbit continues to hop along the river, leaving small prints in the snow, until it disappears in the brush.

"A white one?" Amy answers.

Channing and I smile at each other.

"That's true for now," he says, "but in the summertime, he's brown."

Amy looks doubtful.

"It's true, he's a snowshoe hare. His fur turns white in the winter. It's camouflage to protect him from predators."

"Now that's smart," Amy says.

Channing nods. "Very." He points to the place the rabbit disappeared. "I think his house is in there somewhere."

"Ooo," Amy says, clapping her hands together. "Can we go find him? *Please.*"

"Later," I say. "We need to hide my violin first."

Her disappointment is obvious, but she soon nods and follows Channing the rest of the way across the bridge.

We reach the other side of the river, where it has been mostly cleared of trees. The snow is thicker here. My legs sink with each step as I struggle to keep my violin out of the snow. More and more ice crystals stick to the outer layer of my socks and chill my ankles.

Overhead, clouds ease across the moon; a shadow slips across the barn that sits a ways off from where we walk.

"Look at the lines," Amy says, pointing to a set of tire tracks cutting through the snow behind the barn. The tracks curve and cross in the open field between the barn and the woods beyond.

I stop short while Channing and Amy continue to waddle forward and scan the trees in the distance. When I squint, I spot a metal cattle gate blocking a narrow road that cuts through the woods, and then a black truck parked next to the gate. It must be the truck that left the tracks. My grip tightens on my violin case. God Squad.

I'm about to tell Amy to stop when Channing looks over his shoulder. "It's not them."

My sister spins around. When she notices I'm not following, she runs toward me, the snow crunching with each footfall. Amy pushes her glasses up her nose. "You okay?" she asks and then follows my gaze to the truck. She gasps.

"It's not them," Channing repeats as he nears. "It's the truck Uncle Hyram has me use for chores."

I eye him, unsure.

"You know, for moving bales of hay and chopped logs. Getting gas for the equipment." He shrugs. "That sort of thing."

I gesture toward the gate. "And the road?" I ask, worried the God Squad could be hiding in the woods.

Channing quickly shakes his head. "The road is impassable this time of year." He smiles reassuringly. "Don't worry, I do this every morning. We're the only ones out here," he says, and resumes his march toward the barn.

Amy tugs on my coat sleeve. "I'm sure it's fine if he says it is." She follows him.

"You sure?" I ask, but neither of them answers. They're almost there.

I take a quick breath and hurry to catch up to them. We enter a corral, where horses probably graze in the summertime, and wobble side to side in the enveloping snow, inching toward the barn.

Channing slides open the door and gestures for us to go inside. But it's too dark. My body tenses.

"You first," I say, my voice wary.

He enters the darkness, so dark it swallows him in an instant.

I can hear him walking across something loose, like hay. There's a tiny spark of light from a match, followed by the smell of sulfur. And then a lantern flickers, breaking the darkness and lighting the freckles on Channing's face. He moves across to the other side of the barn and lights a second lantern. And a third and a fourth before he blows out the match.

Amy runs inside toward a pair of milking cows. "Wow. Look at them!"

"You don't have to stand out there," Channing says, and I realize I'm still standing frozen—literally frozen—in the threshold.

Once inside, I shut the door, allowing the warmth to surround me like a thick blanket. My skin tingles as it begins to defrost.

Channing tears off his coat and hangs it on a hook by the horses' stalls. "So why are you so afraid of the dark?"

"I'm not afraid of the dark."

"You sure?" Channing says, tilting his head. "You were pretty upset when they put you in the closet last night, and just now, you wouldn't even come in until I lit the lanterns." He opens a plastic garbage bin that's full of oats. "I figured you were afraid of the dark."

"It's not the dark," I say, my jaw tight.

He takes a shovel full of oats and dumps them into a bucket, hanging the bucket of feed on a post where the horse can reach. "Then what is it?"

Amy pats the neck of one of the cows.

Sweat dampens the back of my neck. "Can we talk about something else?" I ask and place my violin case on a bale of hay before removing my coat.

To my surprise, he nods and turns to Amy. "Would you like to feed them?"

My shoulders relax; Amy nods excitedly.

"Okay, that's this blue bin over here," he says, opening the lid on another container. "I'll put some in their pen in a minute, but you can start feeding them by hand while I finish with the horses."

Amy forms a shovel with both hands. She pushes her fingers into the feed mixture and draws out her hands, dropping bits of grain across the ground as she walks over to the pair of cows. "Here you go," she says, and the first one begins to eat from her hand, its thick tongue slobbering all over her.

She giggles, and I can't help but laugh.

"That tickles," she says.

Channing returns to the horses' feed. "You're doing great."

"What can I do?" I ask.

Without looking at me, Channing says, "You can play for us." He shovels another bucketful of grain.

"But I'm not supposed—"

"To play," he says, finishing my sentence. "I know, but don't you miss it?"

"Do I miss it?" Not as much as I miss the rest of my family, but almost. "What if they hear?"

Channing shakes his head. "Don't worry. We're too far away. They won't."

"But what if they come—"

"I already told you I'm the only one who comes out here."

Amy's hands take another dive into the feed bin. "I miss hearing you play," she adds as she carefully moves over to the second cow, bits of grain slipping through her fingers. "It might make our work go faster if you do."

Channing nods with a sly grin. "I agree. Instead of standing around doing nothing, I think it would be of help if you'd play for us. You know 'idle hands are the devil's workshop,'" he says, quoting the Prophet, but in a way I'd never heard before: in complete jest.

Shocked, I laugh and then quickly cover my mouth.

"Please," Amy says.

My heart beats with possibility. "If-if I did play, what would you want to hear?"

"'Swallow Tail Jig.'" Amy wipes cow spit across her dress. "Definitely."

I shake out my hands and move over to my case, opening it. The honey-colored wood gleams in the low light of the lanterns. Before I can change my mind, I wrap my fingers under the neck and pull it from the velvet. I tuck it under my arm and pluck the strings, turning the pegs to tune each one. Then I grab the bow and place the violin under my chin.

Suddenly, I feel whole again. Like an arm I've been missing for months has been sewn back on.

I place my bow on the string and hear Tanner's voice in my head: *Remember, key of D. Good, clean bow strokes.*

And then I play. Within a few measures, Amy and Channing are clapping with the beat. I glide through the triplet notes. Channing plunges the blade of his shovel into the dirt and dances around the long handle like it's his dance partner. Amy does a jig, bouncing from foot to foot.

The rhythm changes, and the horses bray. Channing abandons his shovel; he bows to Amy. The triplet pattern resumes. She curtsies to him, and soon they're linked arm in arm, spinning and laughing. In the warmth of the barn, I repeat the verse and can't help but wonder why this perfect happiness is so wrong.

14.

Hunched over a box of potato peels, I hum "Swallow Tail Jig" to myself and work the paring knife, removing the skin from another potato. Amy leans back in the kitchen chair, peeler in hand. "When are we gonna look for the rabbit?" she asks.

Behind me, Pearline barks orders at the others. She's given each of us a task for the dinner preparation. Mother drops a bone into one of the boiling pots, preparing the base broth for stew. Others cut vegetables and make biscuits. Pearline walks the kitchen, supervising our progress.

She glares at us. "Hurry. Up." She's already gotten on my sister twice for being too slow. I speed up. When Pearline turns around, I push some of my finished potatoes into Amy's pile, so our piles look more even.

"But what if he decides to move?" Amy asks, pulling a

droopy brown strip from the edge of her peeler and flicking it from her finger.

"Who?" I ask, reaching for the next potato.

"The rabbit," Amy says.

"He won't move," I say, peeling, peeling, careful not to cut my fingers as the potato gets more slippery without the skin. "It's wintertime." I look up, and my sister has stopped again. *"Amy,"* I say, pointing to the half-done potato in her hand.

"Are you sure?" She bobs on the edge of her seat. "Couldn't we go back?"

I take a deep breath, trying to keep my patience. "We will. But we have to finish these first."

With a heavy sigh, Amy returns to work.

"Carrots," Channing announces as he stomps into the kitchen.

I sit up as he enters. He must've just come in from the cold. His cheeks are flushed, and his black coat is covered in droplets of melted snow. "I was told to put these here," he says and dumps the box next to me with a thud.

I eye the box of mounded carrots. My shoulders fall as I realize we're expected to peel these, too.

Amy's face lights up. "Rabbits like carrots, don't they?"

Oh no. Not again.

Channing glances at me and then at her. Smiling, he nods. "I think it's their favorite food."

Amy pokes my hand. "Gentry, we *have* to find the rabbit and give him a carrot."

I shake my head at him. "Thanks for that."

He laughs.

"Enough chitchat," Pearline says to Channing. "They need to get back to work. So do you."

Channing's expression goes tight, but he nods anyway. "Yes, ma'am."

"See ya," he says to Amy and me as he brushes past Pearline. When he's gone, I slide down in my chair. Pearline turns her attention to the group making biscuits. Immediately, she criticizes their sifting technique.

With a sigh, I stand to flip the box on its side so the carrots tumble onto the table. My hands check for rotten ones, when I notice a folded slip of paper among the carrots.

From the impressions on the back, I can tell something's written on the paper. My pulse quickens. I turn to look for Channing, but he's gone.

My hands tremble. I check to make sure Pearline's not looking. Amy's peeling again as I carefully unfold the paper and read it: *Third floor. Brother. ASAP.*

Tanner? Is he here? Or Kel? My heart beats even faster.

"I'll be right back," I say to Amy, tucking the note inside my dress pocket.

Amy nods and keeps peeling the final potato.

When I'm almost out of the kitchen, Pearline snatches my arm. Tight. "Where do you think you're going?"

I clench my skirt pocket, where the note sits. "Um, bathroom," I say. Her face twists in disapproval, but she lets go.

Not giving her a chance to ask more, I turn and run through the living room. The Prophet's eyes seem to follow me from his portrait, as if he knows I've told a lie. I dash past the front door and up the narrow stairs.

When I reach the third floor, I'm out of breath. The hall is empty.

"Tanner?" I whisper. "Kel?"

"Sorry," Channing says, sneaking up behind me, startling me. "Uncle Hyram was blocking the front door. I had to come in around back."

I check the stairs to make sure Pearline isn't following me. "What's going on?" I ask, holding up his note.

Then, the phone rings. Channing grins. "Come on," he says and rushes toward the sound, disappearing inside one of the bedrooms.

I pocket the note and follow him into the biggest bedroom I've ever seen. There's a king-size bed in the center of the room, covered in a diamond-patterned quilt. There's even an attached bathroom. The phone rings again.

"Whose room is this?" I ask, eyeing a box of candy on the nightstand. My mouth waters. I've only eaten candy a handful of times.

"Pearline's," Channing says, and answers the phone.

My throat tightens; I back into the doorway. We shouldn't be here. I turn to leave until I hear Channing whisper, "Tanner wants to talk to you."

At the sound of my brother's name, I spin around.

Channing offers me the phone.

Even though I know I shouldn't be in Pearline's room, I can't miss the chance to talk to my brother. I near Channing and slowly take the phone from him. "H-hello?" I say, tentative.

"Hey, kid," Tanner says with his familiar lilt.

I gasp with excitement. "Tanner! Where are you? How'd you find us?"

Channing smiles and whispers, "I've gotta go."

I mouth *Thank you* to him.

He nods and escapes, leaving me alone in Pearline's room.

"Meryl told me all of you were sent to Uncle Hyram's," Tanner says.

There's a crash downstairs, and I jump. My eyes flash to the doorway—no one. I turn away from the empty hallway, whispering, "You've talked to Meryl?"

"Ever since you were reassigned to Uncle Hyram, Mother hasn't called me. Are you all okay?"

Meryl was right. Mother *was* talking to Tanner.

"Yes," I say. "No." I shake my head. "I don't know. Everything's all messed up. Did you know Kel ran away?"

"He's here with me in Santa Fe."

I manage a breath. "You're in Santa Fe?"

"Yeah, after Uncle Max kicked me out, I hitchhiked here and began sleeping in the Plaza. You know the one where we played?"

I nod to myself.

"I was there about a week before the cops found me."

My mouth goes dry. "Are you in prison?"

Tanner laughs. "No, the cops set me up with Dr. Lawrence and her husband. They took me in."

A woman doctor? "Who's Dr. Lawrence?" I ask, suspicious.

"She's this awesome therapist and counselor."

I shift, suddenly uncomfortable. Why would Tanner need a therapist?

"Kel's here. There are others here from Watchful, too.

Apparently, the Prophet's been cleaning house a lot lately. They call us 'lost boys.' Can you imagine?" He laughs to himself. "Lost boys."

"You sound happy," I admit, even though I don't want to.

"I am, but it's hard. I miss you all so much, and most of the time, I feel so lost and stupid."

"What do you mean?" I ask, spotting the picture of Uncle Hyram next to the candy. I turn the other way.

"Everything's so different out here." He sighs. "I'm happy, but I'm angry, too. I know Mother couldn't do much, but how could Father let him kick me out like that?"

I hear distant footsteps. How long before Pearline realizes I've been gone too long? "Have you heard from Father?" I ask under my breath.

"I tried to call him, but he won't speak to me. Can you believe it? He won't speak to his own son, because he's trying to get right with the Prophet."

I nod to myself. "The Prophet said he might get to come back if he wrote a good enough confession."

Tanner releases a dry laugh. "Like that's gonna happen."

I flinch from the harshness of his words. "It *will* happen," I say, suddenly defensive. "Father's repenting right now." I wipe my sweaty hand on my skirt. "The Prophet will let him come home any day now, and we'll get to return to Watchful. Maybe he'll let you and Kel return, too. We can be a family again."

"I can't come back."

Out of the corner of my eye, I spot someone passing Pearline's bedroom. The phone slips from my fingers, but the person doesn't stop. Still eyeing the doorway, I scramble to bring the phone back up to my ear.

"Did you know the Prophet asked me to spy on Father?"

"What?" I whisper. My chest tightens. I drop to the edge of Pearline's bed, sinking into her soft mattress. Immediately, I can smell her floral soap. I blot my forehead with the back of my hand. "Why would he do that?"

"Because, according to Uncle Max, Father was losing control. For one thing, Mother Lenora told Uncle Max there was tension between her and her sister wives on how to raise the children, and that Father refused to step in."

"Mother Lenora should just mind her own business," I say, feeling protective of Mother all over again. "We were doing fine."

"Not according to the Prophet. 'You can only achieve the United Order if your children are humble and faithful servants of their priesthood head and the Prophet,'" he says, repeating the Prophet's words. Tanner scoffs into the phone. "Whatever that's supposed to mean."

The flowery smell is making me feel worse. "You probably shouldn't make fun like that," I say, twisting the curly phone cord around my finger.

"Shouldn't I? Did you know Mother Dee was sealed to Uncle Max yesterday?"

"No," I say. My stomach twists like the cord around my finger. "What about Father?"

"Believe what I'm telling you: They're never gonna let him back into Watchful."

"Don't say that." I unfurl the cord and stand. I don't want to believe him. I can't. "How do you even know all this when you're out there?"

"Meryl told me when I called, looking for Mother."

My heart sinks. If what Tanner says is true, it has to be so weird for Meryl to be a sister wife to Mother Dee, who was once her mother.

"Now Baby Gwen will only know Uncle Max as her father," Tanner adds. "It's sick."

The Prophet preaches that when a family remarries another man, God changes the children's blood and DNA so it becomes the same as the new father's. He does this so their blood is worthy, and they can gain entrance into the celestial kingdom.

I shake my head. Poor Gwen. Poor Meryl. It can't be true. But why would Tanner lie? "Why are you telling me this?"

"Because I need to get you all out of there before it's too late."

"Too late for what?" I ask, my chest so tight I can hardly breathe. I hurry to straighten Pearline's quilt, trying to remove any evidence I was here.

"The way I see it, the Prophet's rewarding his yes-men with all the wives and subsequently kicking out anyone he views as a potential threat."

All of a sudden, a horrible thought crosses my mind. "Are you saying if we don't leave, Mother might be sealed to someone besides Father?"

"I don't know," he says. "But Mother won't talk to me since you got there. I took a chance *you* might."

"Of course I'll talk to you," I say. "You're my brother." I don't bother to mention the fact that I would've talked to him when we were still in Watchful, too. Especially since I now know he was talking to both Mother and Meryl.

"You know I couldn't talk to you before, right?" he says, like he can read my mind. "They were watching you too closely."

"Watching me?" I ask. I can't help it: I check over my shoulder for Pearline.

"Since we went to the festival together, they figured you'd be the first person I'd try to contact." He sighs into the phone.

"I'm sorry. You have to talk to Mother. I'll feel better when I can get you all out of there."

"But we'll be apostates if we leave," I say, even though he already knows this. Of course he knows it.

Suddenly, Mother calls my name. Her voice is growing louder, closer.

My heart stutters. "Mother's looking for me," I say, getting ready to hang up.

"Okay, but think about what I said," Tanner urges. "Promise?"

"I promise," I say and lower the phone before rushing from Pearline's bedroom.

Mother's winded as she tops the stairs. Her cheeks turn red when she spots me. "What are the two of you doing in there? Where's Amy?"

I shrug. "She's in the kitchen peeling potatoes."

Mother shakes her head. "No, one second you were both there, and the next I turned around and you both were gone. One of Pearline's daughters said she saw Amy stealing a carrot."

Goose bumps rush my arms.

"What are you doing up here, anyway?"

"Rabbit," I say and speed past Mother, down the stairs, almost falling as my heel slips, skipping a step. No time to snatch my coat off the hook, I throw open the door and run past the God Squad guard.

"Gentry, where are you going?" Mother calls from the front door. "We have to get back to the meal prep!"

"I'm getting Amy," I shout and race toward the grove of trees. The snow is blindingly white. I squint as I run; the icy crust crunches beneath my feet. But I don't stop. I keep running. Pushing my legs as fast as they will go, my thighs burning with each footfall. The icy wind whips against my body as I enter the canopy of trees.

Inside the thicket, armlike shadows writhe along the ground. I keep running. "Amy!" I call again.

Straight ahead, I spot the bridge, icicles reaching toward the frozen river below. She's not there.

There's a crackle up ahead and to my right. That's when I spy her through the trees. Walking near the rabbit's den. Another pop. She's standing on the surface of the icy river. "Stop!"

Amy turns to face me, giving a quick smile as she holds up the carrot. Then there's a loud crack, like the sound of a shotgun. The surface of the river gives way; chunks of ice drop into the water. Her face stretches in horror as she falls through the hole with a splash.

"Amy!" I shout and weave through the trees. A branch scratches my face. I pump my arms as fast as I can, racing to the riverbank.

My sister's gasping for air. Her arms thrash, making the

water lap onto the ice. I rush along the windy bank and step out onto the frozen surface. My dress blows around my legs. Before I'm within reach, the ice cracks beneath my feet. I skirt back to the bank. Another crackle. My heart races. "Can you swim to the edge of the hole? Kick your feet."

"I can't," she cries. Her arms splash wildly. She's gasping and wheezing. Water sloshes over the rim of the hole, wetting the surface of the ice. It freezes almost immediately.

"Throw your arms over the side," I say as I whip around, searching for something—*anything*—for her to hold on to. I hurry to the nearest tree. "Hold on," I shout, my voice carried by the stiff breeze. I search for the right-size branch.

She manages to get to the edge of the ice; her body remains submerged. "I can't hold on," she says, throwing one of her arms over the ice.

I keep looking until I find a branch, right above my head. I reach with both hands and jump. My hands skid along the bark as I miss. I barely notice the cutting sting as I jump again and hold tight. Hanging from the branch, I hop, hop, hop. Trying to break it from the tree with my weight. "Come on. Come *on*."

Suddenly, the branch snaps; I fall to the hard-packed snow with a *hrumph*.

Standing on the riverbank, I carefully slide the branch across the ice and lean over the edge as far as I can reach. It's not long enough.

I scan the dark and light patches of ice, weighing my chances. The frozen wind bites my exposed skin. Amy's slumped over. "I can't move," she says. It looks like her sleeve has frozen to the icy surface.

With no time to lose, I drop to the snow on the bank and onto my stomach, trying to spread my weight evenly before I slide across. I slowly inch toward her, shivering with each movement. "Grab the branch," I shout, stretching my arm as far as I can. My hands shake. Blood drips from my fingers and freezes against the ice.

My sister's glasses sit crooked on her face. Her teeth chatter. The branch clicks against the ice as I move it around. Amy grunts, her right hand frantically reaching for the branch. She misses it. A chunk of ice breaks off beneath her arms. She sinks; the water rushes over her head.

"No!" I shout.

She bobs up, managing to throw one arm over the ice. She gasps again. I inch a little closer—another snap—until she finally snags it. "Hold on," I say, my shivering growing worse. I try to leverage my feet, try to find a place to wedge them, but it's no use. It's too slick.

I use every bit of strength I have—my arms burn—until I

manage to pull the branch back enough to draw her onto the ice. The surface crackles under her added weight. It's getting harder to breathe. Like my lungs are filling with snow.

Forcing a sharp breath, I release the branch and slither alongside it before snagging her frozen fingers. "Amy," I say.

Her lips are turning blue. "My legs . . ."

Ice snaps down the river. I have to get us off the ice. With the last of my strength, I manage to roll her onto my body and hold tight. I can hear the ice pop and strain beneath us. One roll at a time, I move us across the surface until we reach the riverbank, landing in the snow.

Amy flops on top of me, and the ice we were on seconds before cracks and dissolves with a splash. It's harder to breathe. I have to get up. Get help. She's like a dead weight. My muscles are too weak to push her off me.

"Amy," I say, but she doesn't respond. I don't know what that means.

The branches overhead blur and twist against the white sky. Someone calls my name. It sounds like my brother. "Tanner," I call. I reach out, but my fingers find only air and snow.

"Can you hear me?" the same voice says as he spins into my vision. Dark hair. Freckles. Green eyes.

"Channing," I say and then try to move. But Amy's body weighs me down. "She needs—warmth."

"Don't worry." He lifts her off me and disappears into the thicket with my sister limp in his arms.

15.

The smell of vegetable stew fills the whole house. Channing helps me sit in the hard dining room chair and rushes away. My wet hair sticks to my face. I'm shivering uncontrollably, but my eyes remain fixed on Amy. It's been at least twenty minutes since Channing carried her to the dining room table, and she's still unconscious.

Channing returns from another room and throws a pile of blankets over my shoulders.

Mother has already removed Amy's glasses and changed her into dry clothes. She now slips a warm water bottle under the blankets, tucking it against my sister's armpit.

"Is she going to be all right?" I ask, but Mother doesn't answer. She looks into Baby Bill's Pack 'n Play, making sure he's still content with his toys, and then returns to Amy.

"Here, drink this," Channing says, carefully handing me a steaming cup of honeyed tea.

I take the warm cup and wrap my shaky fingers around it, trying not to slosh. I breathe in the steam and start melting the ice in my lungs.

"Can I help with something?" Channing asks Mother.

Still, no answer. Mother hurries to the kitchen to retrieve a towel from the oven.

"Is she angry at us?" he whispers.

I sip the tea, avoiding his question. When she's worried, Mother doesn't talk. Which only makes me worry more. I take another sip, allowing the warmth to slowly slide down my throat, and try not to panic.

Mother returns with the heated towel and wraps it around my sister's head before gently lowering her onto the pillow. Amy's chest rises and falls with short, shallow breaths.

Channing rocks from side to side, as if hoping for an assignment.

"She's not warming up fast enough." Mother bites her knuckle as she surveys Amy, then glances at me, then looks at Amy again. "I really think she needs a doctor."

"I'll get Uncle Hyram," Channing says and runs from the room, seeming grateful to have something to do.

Mother paces alongside the table. "What on earth were you girls thinking?"

I flinch between shivers.

She shakes her head, as if trying to think of another remedy. She lifts the towel enough to stroke Amy's matted hair.

Pearline and one of her daughters come into the dining room with dishes and silverware in hand. "We need to set the table for dinner," Pearline says, eyeing my sister on the table.

"Now?" Mother asks.

Pearline nods. "I'll get one of the boys to carry her upstairs."

"You will do nothing of the sort," Mother says. "That may hurt her even more."

Pearline slams the plates on the table. Her daughter drops the silverware with a clatter, as if anticipating an explosion.

I gently slide off the chair, so I can stand next to Mother. My legs shake.

"What seems to be the problem?" Uncle Hyram says, popping a biscuit into his mouth as he strides into the room. He chews it like a cow chews its cud.

"She won't get off the table," Pearline says, her tone sharp.

"That's because she can't wake up," I add, though it comes out less forceful than I'd like.

Mother gives me a look of warning. I take a long drink, hiding behind the teacup.

"Amy was unconscious when I found them," Channing explains.

"I'm so sorry to ask," Mother says as she fusses with the blankets, tucking them under Amy's sides, "but I think she needs a doctor. Can we take her into town?"

Uncle Hyram scoffs, spewing crumbs. "That seems a bit rash to me."

Pearline nods in agreement. I clench my jaw.

"But I can't get her warm," Mother says, her voice quivering.

Uncle Hyram brushes the crumbs from his shirt. "I don't know what you're accustomed to there in Watchful." He crinkles his nose in judgment. "But here in Waiting, we rely on God to heal us."

Mother nods. "Yes, of course, but—"

"If it's God's will, she'll get better." Then he turns to Channing with a cryptic smile. "Don't you have work to do?"

Channing looks startled. "Uh, yes, sir."

"Then get to it. Don't want you undoing all the work you've done because of these girls."

These girls?

With a quick nod, Channing escapes to the living room and then outside. The front door slams shut.

Maybe Tanner's right: Maybe we all *should* get out of here. "Mother?" I ask, willing her to stand her ground and protect Amy.

But Mother wipes a tear from her cheek and nods. "Of course, you're right."

Uncle Hyram lifts his chin.

My shivering has stopped, but suddenly I feel even worse. Especially when I see him coming toward us. I drop the teacup to the floor. It shatters.

Dirk marches into the dining room. My shoulders tighten. What is *he* still doing here?

"Good," Uncle Hyram says, clapping his hands together. "Looks like I'm no longer needed." He points to the floor. "And you, clean that up," he says to me before disappearing into the kitchen.

Pearline turns to Dirk, nodding toward my sister. "Take her upstairs."

"I'll do it," I say, throwing off my blankets as I slip between him and Amy.

Dirk laughs. "You?" He has a smirk on his ugly face. I can smell his rotten breath.

"Gentry, get out of the way," Mother chides. "Go to your room now, and I'll clean this mess."

I blink back tears. "But, Mother." I want to tell her she can't let Dirk touch Amy. Not when he's the one who's always trying to hurt her. He shouldn't be allowed to touch any of us.

"I'm so sorry for her behavior," Mother apologizes to Dirk,

which makes my stomach turn. "I don't know what's gotten into her lately."

"Move," he orders.

My fingernails dig into my hands. I refuse to move.

"Did you give the rabbit the carrot?"

Mother and I both turn at the same time. Amy's eyes are suddenly bright.

"Why am I on the table?" she asks, pulling the towel from her head.

I release the breath I'd been holding.

Mother laughs as she lifts Amy to a seated position on the table, giving her a giant hug. "Oh, my sweet girl. My sweet, sweet girl."

"What's wrong?" Amy asks.

Relieved tears wet my cheeks. Mother keeps one arm around my sister and opens her other arm to me. I fall into her embrace. Baby Bill throws a toy over his Pack 'n Play. Mother laughs and squeezes me. She wipes away my tears. And then her own. "Thank God," she says, and I nod.

Dirk stomps away, seething.

I don't care. *This* is my family. Right here in my arms. What's left of us, anyway. And I think Tanner's right: We have to leave Waiting before we completely come undone.

***

A few days later, in the early-morning hours before dawn, Amy's still too weak to get out of bed, so I navigate the slippery bridge alone. Clouds cover the moon and stars; the sky is a blanket of black. With my arms outstretched, fat snowflakes fall and stick to my jacket. The light from my flashlight bounces against the ice that has formed again along the river, but there's still no sign of Amy's rabbit.

The light beam moves with me across the thick snow, sweeping the wide field and exposing the falling flakes. Behind the barn and beyond the open field, the trees' branches sag from the weight of the snow. Flurries blow against the cattle gate that blocks the narrow road through the woods and stick to the metal, making the gate look like it has a frosty beard. Several inches drift against the tires of Channing's parked truck and cover the hood. The curving tracks Amy and I spotted when we first arrived are now gone, concealed by a blanket of sparkling white.

My legs sink as I attempt to run toward the barn. When I finally reach it, I heave open the door to the warmth and smell of animals.

Channing looks up from his work. "Hey."

"Hi," I say, stomping the snow from my boots. "Can I come in?"

"Be my guest," he says, and returns to milking one of the cows.

I slide the door shut and remove my coat, shaking it out before hanging it on the hook next to Channing's.

I wring my hands, trying to defrost my fingers, while walking over to the place my violin stays hidden between stacked bales of hay. "I never got a chance to thank you," I say, plucking a piece of hay that's sticking out from the top bale.

"For what?" he asks as he milks. Short sprays hit the inside of the bucket at his feet.

"For saving my sister."

"I didn't save her. You did," he says without stopping. "I only carried her inside."

I fidget with the piece of hay for a second and then toss it to the ground. "Thanks for helping, then."

Channing nods with a soft smile. "You're welcome, then," he says, and shifts before standing.

My cheeks flush. I bend over to grab my violin case, and once my fingers find the handle, my body buzzes with a familiar excitement.

"Can I ask you a question?" he asks as he carries a full bucket across the barn with two hands.

I place my case on a waist-high stack of bales. "Sure."

Careful not to spill, he pours the thick milk into an aluminum churn. "Were you scared out there on the ice?"

His question surprises me. I think about it for a half second and nod. "Sure, but there wasn't really much time to think about it."

"Yeah, but weren't you worried the devil would pull you in, too?" he asks matter-of-factly.

I laugh, thinking he's teasing me, and grab my violin by the neck before tucking it between my arm and body.

"I'm serious. You know how the Prophet teaches the devil controls the water."

My smile falls. That's why Mother made us stop fishing together, at least that's the reason she gave me. I shrug. "All I knew was that I had to get to my sister."

"So, you weren't afraid of the devil?"

I shake my head. "I guess not. Why?"

He runs a hand across his mouth. "I just don't understand how someone who's not afraid of the devil can be so afraid of the dark."

I tense and yank my bow from the case. "I'm not afraid of the dark," I say, louder than necessary, and jab my bow through the air, pointing to the barn door. "Obviously, I walked over here in the dark, didn't I?"

"Okay, okay." Channing puts his hands up, as if surrendering. "But what about that thing in the closet when you first got here? You were really upset. I mean, *really* upset."

My mouth goes dry as I try to figure out how to answer. Part of me wants to tell him. But that part's not keeping sweet. If I continue to keep sweet like I'm supposed to, I'll keep it all locked inside forever.

"You don't have to tell me," he says, his voice falling with disappointment as he returns to the cow pen. "I just thought we were friends and that maybe you trusted me."

"I do trust you," I say.

He looks at me like he's expecting me to say more.

I bite my lip.

"It's fine," he says. He moves his short wooden stool beside the second cow. "You were really brave, that's all, and it doesn't make sense to me."

I squeeze my violin tight against my body. "You know those government raid drills we used to have at Watchful Academy?"

He sits on the stool, preparing to milk the other cow, and nods. "Weren't we four or five the last time?"

"Six," I say, my voice quivering a little. I clear my throat. "I was in the bathroom when Uncle Max made the announcement through the speakers, but since there are no speakers in the bathroom—"

"You didn't hear it," Channing says, finishing my thought.

I nod.

He presses his hands against his thighs. "Okay?"

I take a breath, trying to steady my voice. "When I returned to my classroom, no one was there. So I ran and checked my older sisters' classrooms. They weren't there, either."

Channing starts milking the second cow. "We were probably all hiding behind the hidden panels in the basement by then."

"But I didn't know that," I say. All of a sudden, my heart's racing like I'm running through the school again. "I called for my sisters. My brothers. Even Uncle Max. But the panels were soundproof, and I couldn't hear anyone."

Channing stops milking for a second, seeming to put it all together with a nod. "And you couldn't hear us."

"Right," I say. "I ran through the entire school looking, but couldn't find anyone." My hands are shaking, so I lay my bow on the hay. "I was scared and crying. I didn't know what was going on." My shoulders tighten. "That's when Dirk Whittier found me." I move my violin in front of my body like a shield.

Channing's expression darkens.

I force myself to keep talking. "He told me it was the apocalypse and that my family had moved on to the next world without me."

Channing lifts the full bucket as he stands. "And you believed him?" A single line of milk dribbles down the side of the bucket.

"He's the Prophet's son. Plus, he was eleven and much bigger than me," I say, defensive. "I was only six. What was I supposed to believe?"

He nods. "Sorry. Go on." Channing pours the milk into the churn.

I snatch my bow, letting it dangle against my skirt. "I was scared. I thought I'd been left behind." I rock between my feet. "Dirk told me he was sent by the Prophet to come back for me. But first, he had to check the rest of the school for government agents." Tears sting the backs of my eyes. "I told him I hadn't seen any, but he insisted I needed to hide. He said if I didn't, the government agents would find me and torture me."

Channing looks up from his work. He doesn't blink.

I wipe away a tear. "And then, Dirk took my hand."

Channing bristles, dropping the bucket. He knows we're taught boys are snakes, never to be touched.

I swallow hard. "He led me to Uncle Max's office. There's another secret panel that leads to a small cubbyhole in there."

One of the horses brays, making us both jump.

Channing kneads his lips and then whispers, "What did he do?"

I shake my head. "Dirk told me to get in and stay quiet. That my heavenly life depended on it."

Channing clasps his hands on top of his head and begins to pace.

"Dirk left me there. And I was too scared to make any noise. I thought everyone else went on to the celestial kingdom, and I'd never see my family again."

His hands drop to his sides as he stops moving. "I'm so sorry. I wish I knew."

I shrug. "Apparently, after the drill, Uncle Max worked the whole rest of the day with me hidden behind him. He didn't even know I was there."

"How long were you locked in the dark?"

I hug my violin. "Almost ten hours."

Channing shakes his head.

"My family didn't notice I was gone until dinnertime," I say, my voice weakening. I start plucking the strings on my violin and tune them with the pegs. "Anyway, that's why I don't really enjoy getting locked in tight, dark spaces."

"Did Dirk ever get into trouble?"

I let out a sharp laugh. "What do you think?"

"What a jerk," Channing says and then snaps his fingers. "Hey, Dirk the Jerk. What do you think?"

I smile. "I think you're a little late on that one. Everybody's been calling him that since kindergarten."

Channing smiles, tapping a finger against the side of his head. "Thought it sounded familiar," he says and then points to my violin. "How about a request?"

"It depends," I say, tucking my violin under my chin.

He retrieves the dropped bucket. "On what?"

"On whether I know it or not."

"You'll know this one," he says, confident. "'Go, Ye Messengers of Glory.'"

I place my bow on the string, remembering the hymn is in a minor key. I play the simple tune with bold strokes, emphasizing the syncopated rhythm. By the second measure, I can hear Channing lightly singing beneath the rich timbre of my violin. He continues his work around the barn—shoveling grain and watering the horses.

I close my eyes as I play, and the hymn takes me back to so many prayer services in the meetinghouse when my family was still together. My brothers and sisters elbowing one another in their seats. Our mothers shushing us. Father sneaking me a smile. I soon finish the fourth stanza and lower my violin, a little sad it's over.

My eyes open. Channing looks a little sad, too. "It's my mother's favorite." He stops shoveling and wipes his nose with the back of his hand.

I return my violin to its case and tuck it between the bales. "You'll get to see her again soon, right?"

He nods, half-hearted. "That's what Uncle Hyram keeps telling me."

"Then you will," I say with a hopeful smile. "You seem pretty reformed to me."

Channing laughs. "Gee, thanks." And then his smile fades. "Look, I know neither one of us really wants to be here in Waiting." He takes a step closer. My heart flutters. "But I'm really glad we're together." His gaze slips to the hay-covered ground. Even with his hair falling across his face, I can see he's blushing underneath it.

Butterflies flit across my stomach. We're close enough that if I stretch my arm, I could touch his hand.

Then, the barn door flies open with a loud bang. Cold air rushes inside.

Uncle Hyram's eyes flick between us. "What are you two doing in here?" he asks, the vein bulging in the center of his forehead. But it's not really a question. It's an accusation.

16.

"So, this is where you've been going when you sneak out."
Uncle Hyram's eyes narrow and seem to peer right through me.
I struggle to keep the guilt from my face. My heart hammers
inside my chest. He *can't* find out about my violin.

Channing shuffles away from me and grabs his shovel. "She
was just helping me feed the horses, sir."

I nod quickly.

Uncle Hyram looks doubtful as he shakes his head. "Max
warned me about you two." He keeps his gaze of blame fixed
on me.

It's all I can do to resist squirming.

"Now, tell me the truth," he says. "Did this boy kiss you?"

"What?" I ask, my voice upturned with shock. My whole
body flushes hot. "No!"

"Sir, I swear," Channing pleads, his knuckles turning white as he squeezes the shovel. "Nothing happened."

"You've done quite enough, I think." Uncle Hyram nods at Channing. "I'll deal with you later."

I flinch, knowing what that means. Channing turns pale.

And then Uncle Hyram turns to me. "Your mother is looking for you. I suggest you go to her."

But I can hardly process his words. Did he really think we were kissing? What did Uncle Max tell him that would make him think that?

All I've ever been taught is that I'm supposed to remain pure for my future husband. No kissing. Nothing. I know Channing and I didn't do anything wrong, so why is it I suddenly feel so dirty?

"You best hurry inside," Uncle Hyram says.

Humiliated, I turn away from Channing and yank my coat off the hook. I run outside, the sun blinding as it rises along the snowy horizon. My eyes water. But I keep running toward the cabin. Toward Mother.

My breath stutters as I slip on the bridge, but I manage to stay upright before crossing into the skeletal grove of trees. I have to find Mother and tell her nothing happened between Channing and me before the rumor mill starts.

When I reach the massive log cabin, I pass the God Squad guard and throw open the front door. The bitter smell of coffee fills the air. I quickly remove my coat and stomp the snow from my boots before hurrying past the portrait of the Prophet. "Mother?" I call, moving into the kitchen, hoping to find her there helping with breakfast.

Instead, the first person I see is the same white-blond-haired girl who slammed her door in my face the night we first arrived. She gives me a know-it-all smile as she slices a loaf of bread. "I hear your mother's going to marry Uncle Hyram," she says.

What? The smile doesn't leave her face.

My throat tightens as I search the kitchen for Mother. This has to be another trick. If Mother marries Uncle Hyram, all of her children become his. I would have to call him "Father." But I already have a father.

"My father's coming home soon," I insist. "We're going home to Watchful." I nod, trying to convince myself as much as her. "Any day now, we'll be going home."

The girl shrugs. "Whatever you say." She moves on to the next loaf with her knife.

Pearline wipes her hands on a dish towel as she approaches, her long skirt swishing side to side. "Is there a problem?"

I'm so confused. First, I'm accused of kissing a boy for no reason. Now, I'm being told I'll be getting a new father. "Do you know where Mother is?" I ask, my voice shaking.

To my surprise, her face doesn't go tight as usual. Instead, she nods, which makes me even more uneasy. "Up in her room," Pearline says, and then returns to the cooktop to stir the grits.

I dash through the living room and up the stairs, taking two at a time. My hands sweep across the logs as I climb. It can't be true. Mother wouldn't marry Uncle Hyram. She loves Father, and we're going home.

When I reach the third floor, I run down the hallway. "Mother?" I call as I reach our room and then stop.

Amy is out of bed in her nightgown, wrapping shiny white cloth around Mother's arm. Bolts of different white fabrics are spread across the bed. Someone has placed a full-length mirror in our room. Mother spots me in the mirror. "There you are," she says with a twinkle in her eye I haven't seen since before Baby Bill was born.

My heart sinks: It's true. My hands clench as I fight back tears. I open my mouth to speak but can't manage to form the words. I can't believe she's completely giving up on Father—giving up on our family—but here she is, trying on fabrics for a wedding gown.

"This one's my favorite," she says, holding up her arm. "What do you think?"

I glance at Amy for her reaction, and I can tell she's fighting it, too. Her hand swipes a tear from beneath her glasses. She nods weakly.

"Oh, good," Uncle Hyram says, barging in behind me. "You found her."

Amy's eyes go wide as she scurries to cover herself with her pink robe.

I jerk sideways, distancing myself from him as he nods to Mother. He's going to tell her I kissed Channing before I get a chance to explain. "Did you tell her?" he asks.

Mother smiles. "I was about to."

Why does she look so happy? My face goes hot. She could at least *pretend* to be a little less happy about this wedding. "No need," I say, finding the words.

Uncle Hyram's expression turns into a question. "Did you say something?"

I jut out my chin. "Are you deaf?" He is about a thousand years older than Mother, so probably.

"Gentry," Mother scolds.

But I don't care. I whip around to face her. *"You."*

Mother looks startled.

"How could you?" I say, stabbing the air with my finger. "How could you give up on our family?"

Mother smooths her skirt. "The Prophet had a revelation that I now belong to Hyram."

I glare at them both. He's so old and fat. Mother's half his age and still beautiful. I shake my head. "I don't care what the Prophet says."

Mother's expression tightens.

Amy covers her mouth. Silent tears run down her face.

But I can't help it. Any hope of being reunited with our father has now vanished. Our family won't be repaired. If Mother marries Uncle Hyram, I won't even be reunited with Father in the next life.

Uncle Hyram takes a step closer. "Young lady, I expect you to keep sweet in this house."

"I don't care what you expect," I say, even though I know it means a beating's coming. "You're not my father. You'll never be my father." I'm boiling over and can't keep a lid on anymore.

Uncle Hyram nods, smug. "The Prophet was right," he says to Mother. "Conway has completely lost control of his children. No wonder he was banished from the priesthood, and you were sent to me."

"I'm so sorry," Mother says, shaking her head. "She's not usually like this."

"Yes, I am," I argue. "But you make me keep my feelings hidden. All of us. And I'm sick of it!"

Without warning, Uncle Hyram snatches my braid and yanks it firmly upward, bringing sudden, stinging tears to my eyes. "Perfect obedience produces perfect faith." His face shines with sweat.

I try to wrench free, but it only makes the pain worse. My hands fly to my head; his grip stays firm. He twists my braid so tight, I drop to my knees.

Amy's tears are no longer silent. She backs into the corner, whimpering, her eyes full of fear.

"I'm so sorry," I whisper to her.

But Uncle Hyram doesn't let go. "Has she picked a fabric?" Uncle Hyram barks.

Mother's smile is gone. "Not yet," she says and kneads her hands.

He tosses me on the bed. I smack against the mattress, making the bolts of fabric bounce.

"Pick one," he orders.

I cover my hair with my hands so he can't grab it again. My gaze moves between the white cotton and taffeta, the sateen and lace. I don't understand why he wants me to pick the fabric for Mother's wedding dress.

"The Prophet called," Uncle Hyram says, his voice oily.

Mother puts her hands together, as if in prayer. "Thanks be to God."

Amy's blubbering grows louder.

"Gentry," he says, compelling me to look him in the eye. When I finally do, his lip curls on one side. "In one week's time, you will become a wife."

17.

No one knows who I'm supposed to marry. At least, that's what they're telling me. The Prophet had a revelation about my impending marriage, and that's all I've been told. It doesn't matter to me who it is. I can't get married.

The other girls in the kitchen stare and whisper as I take deliberate steps past them and move toward Uncle Hyram's office. I can't get married. I turn the corner, away from the noises of the house—cooking, cleaning, children's cries and squabbles—and meander down the dark and narrow hallway.

I can't get married. My heart beats inside my throat as I reach the closed door at the end of the hallway. I raise my trembling hand to knock.

I could barely look at Uncle Hyram last night when he was sealed to Mother for all time and eternity. I couldn't understand why she was so happy or how she could look so beautiful in her lacy white dress with her hair—like spun gold—woven in a braided crown. How could Mother smile at him or let her cheeks flush pink when he touched her hand? Didn't she love Father anymore? Did the pronouncement of the Prophet really change her heart to where she loved Uncle Hyram instead? He is so old. Even now, the thought makes my stomach clench. My hand falls to my side.

The door flies open, and Channing bumps into me but manages to keep hold of the stack of wood in his arms. "Oh, sorry," he says, his cheeks reddening.

The last time I was this close to him was four days ago in the barn. When Uncle Hyram accused us of kissing.

The back of my neck goes hot. I slip sideways to give him room to maneuver the narrow hall with his load. But he moves the same direction and knocks against me, dropping the logs.

I jump back.

"Oh, sorry," he says again. He looks as nervous as I feel.

"Close the door," Uncle Hyram orders.

Channing reaches for the knob. "Yes, sir."

I step into the threshold, blocking him. "No, please."

The wrinkles on Uncle Hyram's face smooth in surprise and then quickly crease with annoyance. "I'm busy."

Channing squats to pick up the wood behind me, one log at a time.

I wish he'd hurry. I don't want him to hear this.

"Close the door," Uncle Hyram insists.

I swallow hard. "Father," I say, forcing the word from my lips, "I've come to apologize."

Uncle Hyram's expression softens. "Then, do come in," he says, waving me into his office. "Shut the door behind you."

I turn to the door as Channing stands, his arms full again. *I'm sorry,* he mouths, looking like he wants to say more.

Sorry for what? Sorry about my mother and Uncle Hyram? Sorry about my upcoming marriage? Or sorry for something I don't even know about yet? I hug my arms around my body.

"Are you coming?" Uncle Hyram says, and I suddenly remember why I'm here. I softly close the door on Channing.

With a deep breath, I try to focus: I can't get married.

"Have a seat," Uncle Hyram says, gesturing to a pair of straight-back wooden chairs that face his desk.

I sit in the closest one and shift, and shift again, but it's no use. It's as uncomfortable as it looks.

"Who has joined us, Hyram?" a familiar voice says.

My eyes flash to the picture of the Prophet on the wall behind Uncle Hyram's desk. My pulse skyrockets. No, no, no, no, no, no, no!

"It's Gentry Whittier," Uncle Hyram says, using my new last name.

I want to correct him, but I want to get out of here even more. "I-I'm sorry. I didn't—I can come back later." I stand with my hand on the chair to keep from falling.

"No need, child," the Prophet says from the speakerphone. "We've spoken before, as I recall."

My hand squeezes the top of the chair.

"Anything you can say to Hyram, you can say to me."

Uncle Hyram nods to the chair, and I drop into the hard seat once more. I was nervous enough coming to the bishop of Waiting, but now the Prophet? He's the leader of our church—God on earth—and I'm going to tell him his revelation about me is wrong?

"You were saying?" Uncle Hyram prompts, resting his arms on his rounded belly.

I wipe my palms against my skirt. "Um, yes. Uh, I wanted to say I'm sorry about the other night. I was just, uh, surprised and—anyway, I'm sorry."

"Very well," Uncle Hyram says. "If that's all." He stands like he's ready to get rid of me.

I clutch the arms of the chair. I can't get married.

Uncle Hyram returns to his seat. "Is there something else?"

I nod. Come on. Just say it. This is my chance. "I think—I think there's been a mistake."

"What kind of mistake?" the Prophet prods.

Uncle Hyram's expression tightens.

I shift in the chair; it's still no use. "It's just I'm only thirteen," I say and then pause, expecting them to respond with something like they had no idea I was so young and, that had they only known, this never would've happened. But there's only silence.

"And?" Uncle Hyram asks, his voice impatient.

"And I don't think getting married is right for me."

Uncle Hyram's eyes narrow. "Marriage is God's will, spoken through the Prophet."

I scoot to the front of my chair. "Um, I don't mean not ever. Just not right now."

"And you think that's your choice?" Uncle Hyram presses his large hands against his desk. His broad knuckles are turning white. "Are you questioning the Prophet's revelation?"

My heart hammers inside my chest. How can I answer without defying everything I've been taught to believe?

"Have you prayed about it?" the Prophet asks, his voice still calm.

I quickly nod, and it's true. I've prayed lots and lots. I've prayed He won't make me do this.

"Because this is God's calling for your life," the Prophet adds. "Your entire purpose is to please your future husband."

My heart sinks.

"You don't want to be alone for all eternity, do you?"

I shake my head and quickly answer, "No." The thought of losing what's left of my family is unbearable. I've already lost so much.

Uncle Hyram smiles and pushes back from his desk before putting his feet up. He crosses one boot over the other. On the bottom, one of his boots has "Keep" stitched across the sole. The other says "Sweet."

I shudder. "I just don't feel like now's the time," I plead. "If I could wait a few more years."

The Prophet clears his throat. "This is your mission, Gentry. You must open yourself to my revelation. Your eternal salvation depends on it."

So why does it feel like a punishment?

Uncle Hyram crosses and uncrosses his boots. "You should know if you choose to defy the Prophet, you will no longer be welcome to stay here in Waiting."

My mouth goes dry. "Where would I go?"

"You'll be an apostate," the Prophet adds. "No longer chosen or worthy of the celestial kingdom."

I squirm, feeling the trap closing in on me. If I stay, I have to get married. If I refuse to get married, I can't stay. I'll have nowhere to go. Nowhere to live. No Amy.

"God has chosen this path for you," Uncle Hyram adds, and

suddenly I remember Tanner's words: *The Prophet's rewarding his yes-men with all the wives.* I glance at the red folds of skin above Uncle Hyram's collar. My stomach twists in disgust. What if it's him? What if the Prophet says I'm supposed to marry him? It wouldn't be the first time a young girl married a much older man. Just look at Meryl.

"Can you at least tell me who I'm supposed to marry?" I ask, bumbling over my own words. "Maybe if you could tell me who it is, this would be easier."

"Easier?" The Prophet's laughter rings through the phone. Uncle Hyram chuckles, too.

I grip the arms of the chair.

"Patience, child. It will all be revealed," the Prophet says.

Uncle Hyram gives a nod. "Thanks be to God."

***

There's a line of plates along the countertop. When Mother and I reach the last one, she portions a scoop of fried potatoes from her pan. I follow close behind and dip my spoon into the bottom of an oversize can of peaches, until the top of the can is almost to my elbow, and scoop out a slice. It plops and dribbles juice across the final plate, wetting the potatoes.

"Almost dinnertime?" Uncle Hyram asks as he approaches, brushing Mother's hip with his hand.

I swallow hard.

She sets the pan in the sink. "Almost," Mother answers as he kisses her on the cheek.

"Here," I say, shoving the giant peach can against Mother, making her stumble backward. "I'm going to help Amy."

In the next room, my sister carries the silverware in a basket and gives each place at the table a knife, fork, and spoon, precisely situating each one in its proper spot before adjusting to make sure each setting is perfectly straight. She's not even halfway finished.

"Need any help?" I ask.

"No," Amy says. "I've got it."

Uncle Hyram finishes washing his hands, and I know he's going to want to get started with dinner soon.

"You sure?" I ask.

Amy nods, concentrating on lining up the spoon. Mother nears Amy, reaching into the basket. "Here, let me help."

My sister jerks the basket away.

"She wants to do it," I say, blocking Mother's second attempt to reach for the silverware.

Amy nods and moves to the next place on the table. "This is *my* job."

Mother plasters a smile on her face as Uncle Hyram enters the dining room. "But he's ready to eat," she says between clenched teeth.

"And she'll be finished with her job in a few minutes," I say. "Right?"

Amy nods again. "Of course. I do it neater than anyone else, even Meryl."

I smile, remembering how it used to get under Meryl's skin when Amy said that. "You sure do."

In the kitchen behind us, the whole family has started to line up for a plate of food. Boys bump up against one another, elbowing for a better spot. Channing takes his place at the end of the boys. The wives form a single line behind him, followed by the girls.

I near the end of the line. Everybody's staring at Amy, but she's oblivious as she perfectly sets each piece of silverware. I cross my arms over my chest. They'll have to wait.

"This is ridiculous," Uncle Hyram snaps and rushes toward Amy. He rips the basket from her arms. She startles, looking up at him with wide eyes.

"Let me help," Mother says, opening her hands to take the basket.

"It's my job," Amy insists.

"Not anymore," Uncle Hyram says, dumping silverware in

the middle of all three tables with a clatter. "Everyone can find their own tonight." He tosses the basket aside.

My hands clench.

Amy looks to Mother, confused. "But it's my job."

Uncle Hyram's face turns red. "You're too slow."

"She is not," I say, breaking from the line. Some of the girls grumble behind me.

"It's a misunderstanding," Mother says. "Amy likes to set the table when it's her turn. It's just that there's more people now and—"

"This girl's a curse," Uncle Hyram interrupts.

Mother winces.

"She is not a curse," I say, snatching Amy's hand as I glare at him. "You are!"

My new brothers and sisters gasp. Mother covers her mouth as I draw Amy into the living room. Away from them all.

"Am I a curse?" Amy asks, making me stop.

I turn and wipe the tears from her cheeks with my thumbs. "Of course not. You're our greatest blessing."

Amy sniffles. "That's what you say, but everyone else says the devil lives inside me."

"Who says that?" I ask, defensive.

"The other girls." She's having trouble breathing. "They say—that's why I'm so—stupid."

"You're not stupid," I insist. "They are."

Tears run down her face. "They said it would've been better if I died in the river."

"Who said that?" I ask, ready to fight anyone who talks that way about my sister.

"Dirk—and the other boys."

"He's a jerk. Don't listen to him."

"But Uncle Hyram said I'm going to kill Mother with worry." She looks up at me with weak eyes. "Is that true?"

I take her in my arms. She gasps for a breath. I loosen my hold, but don't let go. "Of course not. You make us all happier. If anything, we'll live longer because of you."

"Really?" she asks, her voice full of doubt.

Uncle Hyram stomps into the living room. "Show me where it is," he barks.

Amy stiffens in my arms.

Channing trails Uncle Hyram, his eyes forward. What's going on? Mother's next to enter and everyone else gathers around the fringes of the living room. Watching me. Like they're expecting something to happen.

From the corner of my eye, I see Channing pull a case from behind a pile of firewood. My violin case.

"What are you doing?" I say, but he won't look at me. My chest aches. He's betrayed me.

"You will keep sweet," Uncle Hyram barks, and yanks my violin from the velvet.

I move toward him, eyeing my beautiful honey-colored violin. "Please I'll do anything you say. Please let me keep it."

"You covet this *thing*, when you should obey the Prophet." He holds my instrument by the neck. The only thing I have left of Father. Tanner. My old family.

I reach for my violin, but he smashes it against the stone fireplace before I can stop him. Wood splinters in two. My tears come quick.

"You will learn to obey." He tosses the pieces into the fire. It crackles. Flames lick the wood. "And soon, your husband." Immediately, the honey varnish turns to black. The neck falls away from the body. The strings warp and curl.

Next, he tosses my bow into the fireplace. The blond horse-hairs turn brown and then blacken, filling the room with the smell of burnt hair.

Only then do I realize Amy's holding me, instead of the other way around. Tears wet our faces, but Mother remains fixed in place as she blankly watches our old life burn away.

The faces around me range from confused to pleased, with Dirk's smiling the broadest.

My insides burn and break with my violin.

Uncle Hyram nods at his family before moving his hands together. "Let us pray before dinner."

Out of habit, I bow my head. Amy releases me but remains at my side. I close my eyes and wipe the tears from my face.

Uncle Hyram starts to pray, but I somehow don't hear the words he says.

All I can think is the one thing that truly belonged to me is turning to ash. Without music, I'm trapped. My old life is gone. How did the gaping hole between now and then grow so wide?

I sense someone move in close to me and brush against my left side. The hairs on my arms suddenly stand on end as I smell his rotten breath and lean into Amy.

Uncle Hyram closes the prayer and a clammy hand grabs mine. I open my eyes: It's Dirk.

"What do you think you're doing?" I yell, wrenching from his grasp.

Everyone's looking; finally, I think, he's caught. Finally, people see *his* sin instead of mine.

But some of the girls giggle. Some of the boys shake their heads. Channing's eyes remain on the floor.

I *know* they saw what he did. Why don't they say something?

Uncle Hyram grins as he puts one arm around Dirk and

pushes Amy aside to place one arm around me. I want nothing more than to slip free from the weight of Uncle Hyram's arm. He destroyed my violin. I don't want him anywhere near me.

Mother places her steepled hands against her lips, like she couldn't be prouder.

Suddenly, my heart sinks. I shake my head. No, it can't be.

Uncle Hyram joins our hands, and I feel like I'm going to be sick. "May God bless Gentry and Dirk."

18.

If I'm forced to marry Dirk, it's not only permanent. It's forever. I'll suffer in this life and in the next. How can this be God's will?

"You two make a beautiful couple," Mother says from our bedroom floor as she rolls the silky white fabric she picked for my wedding dress and pins the hem.

"We're not a couple." I cross my arms over my chest, my eyes red and puffy in the mirror. "I can't stand him."

"Put your arms down," she says, crawling around me to fold the next section. "I don't want the hem to be crooked." She adjusts the delicate fabric. "And don't say that."

My arms fall to my sides. "I can't marry him," I say, pleading to her stooped reflection. "Remember, you said I was too young to get married?"

Mother shakes her head. "I said no such thing."

"But you did," I say, desperate for her to remember. "When Meryl said I could be next, you said thirteen was too young."

"You should trust in the Lord." Mother finishes and stands, her fingers sorting through piles of ribbon and lace. "You should feel honored to be engaged to the Prophet's son. To have the privilege of being his *first* wife. You don't have any other choice."

I bite my bottom lip. It's painful to hear her say it. But what did I expect? She said the same thing to Meryl.

She said nothing when Uncle Max threw Tanner out of Watchful. She said nothing when the Prophet reassigned us to Uncle Hyram and then told her to remarry. She said nothing when Uncle Hyram smashed and burned the one thing that meant something to me. For her, the priesthood and the Prophet always before anything else. Religion over family. No matter what.

But she's right about one thing. I wipe my eyes. If I don't marry Dirk, there are no other choices. I'll be a thirteen-year-old girl with no family and no place to live. "You're right, I don't have any other choice," I concede.

Mother puts a hand on my wet cheek and smiles softly. "Good girl." Then she removes a couple of the pins between my shoulder blades and comes between the mirror and me, carefully slipping the dress from my body. As Mother slides my wedding gown over a dress form, I put my simple cotton dress on over my sacred underwear.

"It will be ready for you to try on tomorrow morning before the wedding," she says, admiring her work.

A wave of nausea crashes inside my stomach. I can't marry Dirk. Not tomorrow. Not ever.

"We can make any tweaks to the fit then."

I crook my arm behind me to reach the zipper along my back. I need air.

Mother touches my shoulder. "Here, let me," she says, helping to zip me up. She lifts my long braid and twists it into a bun. "You know, I've heard Dirk thinks your hair is really pretty. How do you want to wear it tomorrow?"

Gall rises and coats my tongue. The thought of using my hair—the hair I've been growing since birth—to wash Dirk's feet in heaven makes me gag. I quickly shake my head. "Whatever you think." I have to get out of here. I swallow the bitterness, willing myself to keep it down. "May I go now?"

She nods. "You're going to make a beautiful bride."

I dash through the hallway and hurry downstairs, snatching my coat from the hook and, without stopping to put it on, run outside beneath the gray sky.

The cold air feels like a slap in the face, but I take a deep breath anyway, trying to burn away the nausea. With a quick nod at the guard, I tug on my coat and hurry toward the thicket.

"Where do you think you're going?" a voice I detest asks. Dirk emerges from the side of the house.

My shoulders tighten as he marches after me, the snow crunching beneath his boots. I don't stop. "For a walk," I say without turning around or slowing.

I can hear him closing in on me when, out of the blue, he snatches my hand with his scarred one. I try to tug away from him, my feet sliding against the packed snow. "Let go of me."

"You're going to be my wife," he says, squeezing harder, shooting pain through the top of my hand. "I can do anything I want."

"Please," I say with another tug. "You're hurting me." I yank again.

But it's no use. He's too strong.

Dirk sneers at me for a second. "If you remain faithful, God will change your feelings about me." He finally lets go.

I stumble backward and hold my hurting hand against my stomach. Never, I think. I will never ever feel different. I hate you. I hate you. I *hate* you.

"You will be obedient like the Prophet commands," he says. "I'll make sure of that." Then he gives me a wink, followed by a cruel smile. "See you tomorrow." He heads in the direction of the house.

I smear a stray tear from my cheek and turn, running toward the river. The cold air stings my face as I slip between the trees.

My feet slow as I near the bridge. I hear a snap up ahead and spot Amy in a giant tree that overlooks the river. Her legs dangle over the bare branches, her lavender dress flapping in the wind. She leans against the trunk with a carrot in her hand.

I wipe my eyes and nose, so she doesn't see I've been crying again. Even though the sun is strong and has melted the river along its shallow edge, it's still cold. The wind swirls around my neck, making me shiver. I draw my hood over my head to block it. "Find him?" I call to my sister, knowing she's looking for the rabbit.

Amy sighs, her breath forming a cloud in front of her face. "Not yet," she says before gracefully climbing down the tree. She makes it look so easy.

When she lands on the soft snow beside me, I can see the tips of her ears are pink from the cold. "Here," I say, reaching for the hood on her coat, pulling it over her head. Face-to-face, I spy the dark circles under her eyes. She didn't sleep last night, either. "Better?"

Amy nods and longingly searches downstream with her eyes. The wind rustles the trees, making them groan and click along the shore.

"I know it's wrong," she says, her voice barely a whisper.

I shake my head. "There's nothing wrong with looking for that rabbit. You'll find him when he's ready."

"That's not what I mean." She takes in an extra breath like she's having trouble catching it. "It's just . . . I don't want you to marry Dirk."

"Amy . . . ," I say, wishing I could protect her from worry. But what can I say? I'm scared, too.

My sister twists the carrot tightly between her fingers. "I know it's selfish."

I shake my head.

"Following the Prophet's will is supposed to fill your heart with God's love, but I still don't want you to marry him." Her breath shudders as she drops the carrot inside her coat pocket. "I'm sorry I'm having mean thoughts."

I touch the sleeve of her jacket. "You don't have a mean bone in your body."

She rubs her lips together—like she's not sure whether she should say any more. "Dirk does, though," she whispers. "He's really mean."

"He is," I agree. It's no use denying it. She'd know I was lying, and I'm not going to do that. Not to her.

Amy's bottom lip quivers. "I don't want you to live with him in another house."

I wrap my arms around her.

Her shoulders shake. "I don't want you to go into hiding, where Channing can't find you."

I pull away, shocked. "What did you say?"

Tears roll down her pink cheeks. "Then I'll have to stay here with Mother."

"Where'd you hear we're going into hiding?"

Amy's head falls against my chest. "I overheard Uncle Hyram telling Mother," she says, her voice muffled against my coat. "It's not fair."

I should've realized it before. But in all the mess of learning I'm supposed to marry Dirk, I've only focused on the fact I'll have to be with him every day of my life, and in the hereafter. I haven't even thought about *where* we would live. I didn't even realize this would break the last of my family away from me. I'll be alone. I clench my jaw to prevent the tears from flowing.

Footsteps crunch the snow, and over the top of Amy's head, I spot Channing heading straight for us. I stiffen. For a second, my anger—for his betrayal in handing over my violin to Uncle Hyram—overtakes my sadness.

"Come on," I say, spinning my sister toward the trees. "We'll look for the rabbit later."

"Hey," Channing says.

Amy turns to wave, but I push down her hand. "We're ignoring him," I say, willing her to keep moving. Thankfully, she follows my lead.

"Wait," Channing calls.

"No!" Amy shouts, still walking. "We're ignoring you."

He laughs. "You're what?"

I whirl around to face him. "Don't you *dare* laugh."

The smile immediately leaves his face.

"Leave us alone."

He shakes his head. "Gentry, I'm so, so, so sorry about your violin. I didn't know he was going to destroy it."

"I don't care what you *say* you knew," I say, angrily poking my finger through the icy air.

Channing looks at Amy. "Do you mind giving us a minute?"

My sister gives me a sly smile. "Sure," she says with a nod. "Okay."

My cheeks flush. "You don't have to leave just because he asked."

"I know," she says and then walks toward the house anyway.

I cross my arms over my chest.

When she's gone, Channing points in the direction she left. "People underestimate her."

"Don't you forget it," I say, the sadness seeping in again and mixing with the anger in my gut. Who will defend her if I'm not around? A few days ago, I would have asked Channing to look after Amy, but now I know I can't trust him.

He puts up his hands. "Look, I only told Uncle Hyram about your violin because he thought we were sneaking off to the barn to kiss."

"That's ridiculous," I say.

For some reason, he suddenly looks hurt.

But I don't care. "Why would Uncle Hyram think that?"

Channing shakes his head. "I don't know, but I had to tell him the real reason why you came out to the barn." He wipes his hands across his pants. "I thought I was protecting your honor by telling him about your violin."

"*My* honor?" I say.

He nods. "He didn't believe me. So, I had to show him your violin to prove it."

"Oh, sure. Right before he smashed it and burned it."

Channing flinches. "What choice did I have?" There's an edge to his voice. "He told me I'd never see my mother and brothers and sisters again, because I'd defiled you."

"And I'm supposed to feel sorry for you?" I slap my hand against my chest. "I've lost my father, my brother, my sister, my mother, and by tomorrow, pretty much my entire family. You want me to feel sorry for *you*?"

He shifts between his feet. "I guess I didn't think of it that way," he says. "I was so focused on seeing my family again, I didn't stop to think."

"You sure didn't," I say, anger rising. "While you're happily reunited with your family, mine is being taken away." My fists clench, thinking of the way Dirk squeezed my hand. "And I'm being forced to marry the biggest jerk on the planet."

Channing smiles slightly. "I thought *I* was the biggest jerk on the planet."

I scoff, forming a cloud before my face. "For once, I think you might be right."

"Then let me try and make it up to you," he says, pulling a folded piece of paper from his pocket.

"What's that?" I ask, wary.

"I know it won't give you back your violin, but maybe it can help," he says, offering it to me.

I shake my head. "I don't want any help from you."

"Please, take it," he says, nudging the air with the paper. "Maybe if you call Tanner, he can sneak you out of Waiting."

Despite myself, my heart flutters with hope. "Tonight?"

Channing shifts. "Next week at the earliest, maybe."

Disappointment steals my last hope. "By next week, I'll be"—I stop myself and swallow hard forcing myself to say it—"married. I'll be married, and then who knows where I'll be?"

His expression changes. Like he didn't realize I'd be leaving

Waiting. Channing straightens and nudges the paper toward me. "Call him anyway. Maybe he'll have an idea."

I shake my head. "It's no use."

"You're just gonna give up?"

Heat rises along the back of my neck. I snatch the paper from his fingertips and barely glance at the writing. "How do I even know this is Tanner's number? How do I know it's not some kind of trick?"

Channing's shoulders sink, but I don't care. I can't trust him. He proved that when he handed over my violin. I quickly rip the paper and toss the pieces into the air, letting the wind carry the scraps up and away through the bare branches.

"What's going on here?" Uncle Hyram yells, startling us both. He charges through the barren trees.

I edge away from Channing.

Uncle Hyram's broad fingers reach and snatch one of the paper shreds midair. He scowls as he looks at the indecipherable pencil-scratch. "What's this?" he asks me.

My heart thuds, but I manage a shrug. "Don't know. I didn't read it," I say, which is true. I hardly looked at it before I ripped it up.

"Channing?" he asks, his tone accusing.

Channing fiddles with the zipper on his jacket. "It's nothing, sir."

Uncle Hyram presses his lips into a thin line, glaring at us, waiting for one of us to crack. When we don't say anything, he thumbs toward the house. "Gentry, stay in the house the rest of the day and pray about what you've done."

"Me?" I ask. "But I didn't do anything."

Channing nods, a little too hard. "We were just talking, sir. Nothing more."

Uncle Hyram shakes his head, looking unconvinced. "Are you not an engaged woman?" he asks me. I don't respond, but he continues, "It's plain shameful for you to be accepting love notes from another man."

Love notes? My insides boil. "I didn't."

Uncle Hyram's eyes narrow. "You must think about your family and how this reflects poorly on us."

"You're not my family," I say.

His expression tightens. "You will go inside. You will fast and pray the rest of the day. And don't even think about having that imbecile sister of yours sneak you any food."

Even though I can sense his rising fury, my anger is stronger. I open my mouth, but Channing beats me to it. "Amy's not an imbecile," he says and then adds, "sir." He smiles at me when he says it.

Without warning, Uncle Hyram's energy spins toward Channing. He punches him in the face.

I flinch as Channing drops to the ground. "Are you okay?" I ask, crouching near him.

But Uncle Hyram shoves me backward into a tree, sending shards of bark flying from the impact. Pain shoots down my arm. I stumble forward and grab and rotate my shoulder to make sure I can still move it. It's sore, but I can.

"I warned you to stay away from her," Uncle Hyram says as he snags Channing and drags him toward the river. Even though he's big enough, Channing doesn't fight back. Why doesn't he fight back?

Channing's heels leave tracks in the snow. My heart races.

When they reach the edge of the river, Channing's body remains limp along the riverbank. Uncle Hyram grabs him by the hair and suspends his head above the icy water.

"Gentry," Uncle Hyram growls. "I told you to go inside."

My feet crunch the snow. "No, please! We were only talking."

"Go, now," Channing murmurs. "I deserve this for what I've done."

I shake my head. "You didn't do anything."

Channing pleads with his eyes. "I don't want you to see this."

I take one step backward.

"Please," he says, and I turn to run toward the house. Right before the splash and rush of water, followed by his sharp gasp.

19.

Moonlight filters through the curtains, turning our room a darker shade of blue. Amy snores softly next to me. Her coat hangs from the foot of our bed.

She tried to sneak me food, exactly as Uncle Hyram predicted, but the carrot she'd originally intended for the rabbit still sits inside her coat pocket. I didn't want to get her into trouble, too.

My stomach rumbles with hunger. My eyes remain open, probing the surrounding darkness. The dress form with my finished wedding dress draped over it stands guard next to our bedroom door like a stiff ghost.

It's Mother's night with Uncle Hyram, which—no surprise—he refused to change. *It's high time she grew up and learned to live without her mother,* he'd said, *because tomorrow she's going to be someone's wife.* In response, Mother asked Pearline to keep Baby Bill so that I could get my "beauty rest" before the wedding. I almost laughed when she said it. Like I cared how I looked for Dirk. Besides, I couldn't sleep even if I wanted to.

My mind reels for a way out of this mess. I can't stop thinking about Tanner. Offering the possibility of escape sometime next week. And Channing. How he covered for me when I ripped up Tanner's number. And, finally, Dirk. How I know, in my gut, I'm not supposed to marry him. That if I marry him, I'll be miserable forever. And if he takes me into hiding, I may never see my family again.

My mind spins the other direction, knowing if I leave the community, Mother will be disgraced. I'll become an apostate—forbidden from ever returning to the only home I've ever known.

But something deep inside keeps telling me the Prophet's revelation is wrong. *So, so wrong.* I can't imagine God wanted my family to end up so fractured. I can't understand how I'm supposed to be happy when I'm being forced to marry someone I don't choose.

Someday, I want to be a wife and mother. At least, I think I do. But, for now, I want to be a girl who can dream. I want to live with the possibility I can make some of those dreams come true. And in order to do that, I know there's only one solution: I can't marry Dirk.

I have to leave. Tonight.

I sit up in bed, letting the covers fall to my waist. Careful not to wake Amy, I shift from under the sheets and hurry to get dressed in the bluish light. I pick my heaviest cotton dress and fumble to slip on my three pairs of socks—a light stocking, followed by two heavier ones—over my sacred underwear and slide on my boots.

Once dressed, I rush to Amy's side of the bed. She's still snoring peacefully. I hate to wake her, but there's no time to lose. Not now.

I drop to my knees and shake the mattress. "Amy," I whisper. "Amy, wake up."

It takes her a second to stir, but her eyes soon pop wide open. I place my finger over my lips, willing her to listen before she speaks. She reaches over and slaps the nightstand in order to find her glasses.

She slides them over her ears uneasily. "You're all dressed," she whispers.

I nod. "There's not much time, and I'm so sorry to do this right now, but now's my only chance."

Lines of worry crease her brow.

I take her hand and squeeze. "I can't marry Dirk." I shake my head. "I just can't do it. I know the Prophet says I should marry him. But I don't love him. I don't even *like* him."

"Me neither," Amy agrees.

"I have to leave." I squeeze again. "And I'd like to take you with me."

She sits up.

"I'll understand if you want to stay," I quickly add, trying to keep my voice steady, trying not to reveal how much I want her to come with me. "If you leave, it would mean leaving Mother and Baby Bill and everyone else in the community."

"Forever?" she says.

I nod. "Forever."

She fiddles with the delicate lace collar Mother sewed onto her nightgown. "But if I stay, I'd never see you again."

I knead my lips before answering, "Probably not."

Amy looks deep in thought and then, after a second, she grins. "You kept your promise," she says.

I don't understand.

"You promised you'd never leave me, remember?"

I smile. "You're my partner in crime. I can't leave you." I shake my head. "But this really isn't my decision. You have to decide if this is what *you* want." I take a deep breath and stand, trying to calm my nerves. "It's time we start making our own choices for a change."

Amy throws back the blankets, and then her feet hit the carpet. "Help me get dressed."

My mouth splits into a wide grin. I'm so happy, I could explode. But it's way too early to celebrate. We still have to get out of the house undetected, past the God Squad, and through the gate. And then, who knows how we'll reach Tanner?

While Amy digs through a drawer for her sacred underwear, I find her blue corduroy dress in the closet. "Here," I whisper as I hand it to her and turn away, so she can change. I search through Mother's drawers until I find two of her knit wraps. I pull one around my shoulders.

I can hear Amy slip her coat on over her dress and turn to find her fully clothed. I hand her the heavier of the two wraps. "It's really cold out there. Put this over your head and ears," I say, reaching for the doorknob.

"What are you doing?" Amy asks, whisper-shouting.

My fingers slip from the door as I state the obvious: "Leaving."

Amy shakes her head. "We can't go through the front door. Uncle Hyram knew you were sneaking out to the barn when you went that way, remember?" She points to the window.

My stomach sinks. She's right, though the thought of climbing down from our third-floor window doesn't sound much better.

"Grab another scarf for your head," she says, and then moves to the window. I dig through the drawer for Mother's only other scarf. When my head's wrapped, Amy opens the window; we both shiver from the sudden blast of cold air. I wish I had my coat.

My sister turns her head from side to side, craning her neck. "There," she whispers, and points. I stick my head out of the window, too. The icy wind makes my eyes water. I rub away the tears so I can see what she's found: a steel downspout that runs from the roofline rain gutter and down the side of the house.

My gaze follows the drain. It's a long way down.

"I'll go first," she says before I can stop her.

My heart races as she shimmies her upper body outside the window. What was I thinking, asking her to do this? What if she falls and hurts herself? Or worse?

"Be careful," I whisper, but she's already reaching for the drainpipe with her right hand, her left still holding the windowsill. Her hand grasps the pipe as she swings one leg out of the window, letting it dangle. She moves with confidence, like when she's climbing trees. The toe of her boot finds a crook between the logs. When she gets both hands on the pipe, she uses the logs as stairsteps, slowly descending each one until she reaches the snow-covered ground. My chest swells. She makes it look so easy.

Amy grins, gesturing for me to join her. She doesn't even look winded.

I glance one last time at the silken wedding dress Mother made for me and wipe my hands on my skirt. My fingers latch on to the windowsill as I slide my upper body outside the window, trying to mimic my sister's movements. The frozen air stings the exposed skin on my face and hands.

"Grab the drainpipe," Amy whispers up to me.

I stretch until the tips of my fingers touch the metal and then slip against the ice. My heart races. How did she grab hold with it being so slick? Then I notice: It isn't icy everywhere—only in certain spots.

Wiping my hand on Mother's wrap, I try again. This time, I manage to grip the drain with one hand and carefully drag my right leg out of the window, letting it dangle and bump against the house. I don't dare look down as my foot clumsily brushes against the logs and finally finds a toehold.

Suddenly, a light pops on a few windows away from ours—Pearline's. My foot slips free of its notch. Amy ducks behind a holly bush. With one leg in and one leg out of the house, I struggle to find another place for my dangling foot. My right hand clasps the pipe, while the fingernails on my left hand dig into the windowsill. My shoe kicks against the logs.

"Lean and swing," Amy instructs. With a breath, I release the window and swing my upper body toward the drainpipe. My left hand smacks the pipe, sending a shot of pain through my fingers as they curl around the metal. My other leg slips from the window and thuds against the house.

The curtains fly open. Pearline stares out her window. My heart races.

Amy dips deeper into the shadows. I press my body as close to the house as possible, but my arms are shaking. The wind swirls around me. Part of Mother's scarf flies free and whips behind me like a flag, signaling my location.

With all my strength, I hold on to the pipe with one hand and quickly snatch the loose scarf and yank it from my neck, letting it drop to the snow. With my head exposed, the cold pricks the back of my neck and nips my earlobes. My muscles tremble. I don't know how much longer I can hold on.

The curtain suddenly closes. The light goes off. I wait a second. Two seconds. Three.

Amy peeks from between the sharp-edged holly leaves. "I think she's gone."

My hands loosen, and I slide down the pipe, my feet too frozen to find the notches like Amy did. I drop with a *hrumph*, a snowdrift padding my landing and surrounding my legs like an icy pillow. My lower back aches from the fall, but with no time to waste, I retrieve Mother's scarf from the ground, shake it out, and wrap it around my head—tighter this time. But now it's wet with snow, chilling my already frozen ears.

Back on my feet, I limp-run to Amy and snatch her hand.

"That was a close one," she says as we navigate down the steep driveway and slip-slide toward the gated entrance to Waiting.

We move quickly, but the sound of snow beneath our boots is too loud. The moon is too bright, exposing us to the world—two moving dots against a sheet of white. I consider changing our path so we can use the trees to our left as cover, but that will take us longer and I'm already getting numb from the cold.

Amy suddenly wheezes next to me, her hand limp inside mine. Our strained breath appears before our faces. I can feel us slowing, and as we move the last few feet, I'm beginning to wonder whether we'll be able to jump the fence quickly enough if we encounter the God Squad.

As we round the bend, I snap my arm straight in front of her, stopping us both. My feet slip a little on the slick snow. "Let me check," I whisper and slide a bit more, so I can check the gate.

It doesn't look like anyone is guarding it. I breathe again and wave for Amy to join me. When she does, we slowly approach the entrance to Waiting.

"It's unlocked," Amy says, pointing to the dangling padlock.

With my numb fingers, I pull on the frozen chain link. The gate rattles and easily opens. Too easy.

"What's wrong?" she asks.

Channing said they usually work the fence line at night. My eyes dart and search the darkness, looking for the God Squad.

I hear them before I see them. Tires press against the snow. I snatch Amy's elbow. "Come on," I say and drag her toward the trees. But it's too late. A pair of headlights appears from the direction of the house and shines at our backs. I dart sideways. We're almost hidden by the thicket when I trip on a branch and fall. "Keep going!" I shout.

But Amy returns and ducks to help me.

"What are you doing?" I ask, trying to push her back into the trees.

"You don't leave me. I don't leave you." She pulls me up as a blackened figure jumps from the running truck. My pulse races. My ankle throbs. Blinded by the headlights, I can't see his face.

"I won't marry Dirk!" I shout and turn toward the trees. Amy squeezes my hand.

"Are you *trying* to wake everybody?" a hoarse voice asks as he moves in front of the headlights.

I squint. Channing?

"Channing," Amy breathes with a smile.

As he staggers toward us, I can see the bruises marring the left side of his face. "It's a trap," he says as he reaches us, his voice raspy. Like he has a cold.

On instinct, I fearfully glance behind my shoulder and into the trees.

"There's God Squad posted down the road and in town. They're waiting for you."

I stiffen, still unsure whether I can trust him. "How do you know this?"

Channing shrugs and then winces from the pain. "I heard Uncle Hyram talking to Dirk about it. I guess they thought I was still passed out."

I shiver.

He sighs an icy breath. "They knew you were going to try to escape."

"How?" I ask, doubtful. "I didn't even know."

Channing smiles a little. "Didn't you?"

Amy nods. "It doesn't take a genius to figure that one out."

I glance between them, still uncertain as my gaze lands on Channing's bruised face. "Why are you telling me this? Aren't you worried about getting into even more trouble?"

"It doesn't matter anymore." He shakes his head. "I'm leaving Waiting."

My breath lurches. "What about your family?"

Channing nervously runs his fingers through his dark hair. "I think I finally realized Uncle Hyram was never going to let me go." He looks past the fence. "My best chance is to try and find them out there on my own."

Amy nods. "Good for you."

"Thanks," he says and then clears his throat. "Anyway, we can't go out the main gate or they'll catch us before we even go a mile."

My stomach clenches. "But we can't . . . stay," I say, my voice catching on the last word.

Channing points back up toward the house. "We need to go that way."

Amy grabs my hand.

I quickly shake my head. We just escaped and he wants us to go back?

"It's the only way to avoid the God Squad. It will take some extra time, but if we can get past the house and then behind the barn, we can take the road."

I suddenly remember the long-hidden tracks in the field behind the barn and the cattle gate. "The back road?"

He nods.

Doubt tugs at me. "I thought you said that road was impassable in the winter."

His lips curl into a sly smile. "For them, maybe. But not when you're prepared."

I glance at his truck and notice the silver chains on the oversize tires.

"And they don't know it like I do," Channing adds. "On and off since the first snowfall, I've been going farther and farther into the woods. I know every drift and downed branch."

"Where does the road lead?" I ask.

He makes a big circle with his finger. "The long way around town until it eventually connects with the highway." Channing's arm drops to his side. "It'll take an extra hour or so to get through the woods and past where they'll be waiting, but it *will* work."

Amy nervously squeezes my hand. "Someone could still see us from the house before we get there."

"She's right," I say with a nod. "Or what if someone's already milling around?" The thought makes me shudder. I check over my shoulder but see only more snow and trees. I face Channing and take a breath, attempting to calm my racing heart. "It'll look pretty suspicious: the three of us riding around in your truck."

"No one will see you," he says and then gives me a nervous glance. "If you're willing to hide in the back under the cover."

Amy releases my hand. "In the bed of the truck?"

My muscles tighten on instinct. "Forget it." I was able to get out of Watchful without hiding in the back of Tanner's truck. "We can hide behind your seat and—"

"Won't work," Channing says, cutting me off.

"I've done it before," I argue. "Under a blanket."

"There's not enough room for both of you," he explains.

Amy shivers and gives me a worried look. Her eyes water from the cold. "I don't want to ride in the back alone."

"You won't," I say and rub my sister's arms, hoping to comfort her and keep us both warm. If only I could think of another way out.

A twig snaps behind us, making us all jump.

I spin around. Amy shrieks with joy. Between a pair of bald trees, the white rabbit stands on his hind legs, his long ears twitching. My sister nudges me with a whisper, "He's come to say good-bye."

"I think you're right," Channing says under his breath. He smiles. "Don't you have something you want to give him?"

Amy looks confused for a second. I smile and nudge her side to remind her. She trembles with excitement and plunges her hand inside her coat before pulling the carrot from her pocket.

The rabbit's nose twitches.

Amy tosses the carrot a few feet away from us; it lands softly in the snow.

Dropping to all fours, the rabbit hops to Amy's gift and, after giving it a quick sniff, begins to nibble.

"We better go," Channing says, moving toward his truck. "We want to be long gone before the sun comes up."

Amy doesn't move. "Good-bye, rabbit," she whispers and then takes my hand.

We stay that way for a second, watching him eat, until I gently tug her toward the running truck.

The exhaust curls around us and makes me cough. Channing pops the back. Amy jumps up and slides across the truck bed, pushing aside gas cans and a snow shovel before huddling under a quilt.

"I'll let you out as soon as it's safe," Channing says and then raises a hand. "Promise."

"It's warmer here," Amy says.

I eye the dark space and the lid that will trap us inside. My pulse thrums as I think of being locked inside Uncle Max's cubby all those years ago by Dirk. I'd been forced to hide. I was alone.

Amy smiles. "You coming?" she asks.

This time feels different. With a nod, I quickly jump up into the bed of the truck and slide in next to my sister.

"Watch your head," Channing says as I wrap my arms around Amy, sharing her warmth. We duck. He gives me a wink. "See you on the other side."

The space goes dark as he lowers the cover. Amy throws the blanket over me, too. The lock latches.

I tuck my nose beneath Mother's scarf, breathing in her smell. To my surprise, I'm suddenly more tired than scared.

The tires press against the snow as we move, and after several minutes, my sister whispers over the hum of the engine, "Gentry?"

"Yes?"

She shifts against my side. "Do you think we'll ever see them again?" I know she's talking about Mother and Baby Bill.

I hold her tight, reminded of Father's story about the boy who left his family and could never return to them because the gorge was too large to cross.

"We can try," I say, and kiss the top of her head.

Maybe instead of concentrating on the giant hole that seems too deep and wide, we can look for the bridge instead.

It may take us a long time to find it. It may not. But, with some work, we may be able to find our way back home.

20.

One Month Later

I sit in the hairstylist's swivel chair. Beneath the black cape, my fingers tug the knees of my jeans. Long, red hair clippings mix with my sister's blond cuttings on the linoleum floor. The hair dryer blows hot air across my neck and makes the red and pink hearts taped to the ceiling sway back and forth.

Dr. Lawrence, the woman who's helping Tanner and the other lost boys (and, I guess, the lost girls now), explained to us that Valentine's Day is a holiday about love.

Amy puffs her breath, making her freshly cut bangs fly off her forehead. Dr. Lawrence adjusts her red glasses. She sits next to my sister and gives me a thumbs-up. "Looking good," Dr. Lawrence says.

Amy stops fiddling with her bangs and sneaks a peek.

"Definitely," she says. I move my hands from my jittery knees to the arms of the chair and squeeze, hoping they're right.

Dr. Lawrence snaps her fingers. "Oh, I almost forgot to tell you: Channing called. He made it to Colorado last night, and with any luck, he'll find them today." Dr. Lawrence hired a private investigator who found Channing's family in the mountains outside of Denver.

I breathe, happy he's finally getting the chance to be reunited with his family. "That's good news," I say, though I can't help but worry.

"Either way, I asked him to call tonight." She gives me a reassuring smile. "I'm sure he'll be fine."

Amy shakes the candy box before popping another pastel heart in her mouth. Dr. Lawrence turns to my sister. "What did that one say?" Amy shrugs in response, and Dr. Lawrence wrinkles her nose. "You're supposed to read them to me first, remember?" Dr. Lawrence is trying to help us all catch up with reading and writing and math, so we can start school next fall. It's not much time, but Dr. Lawrence is confident we can do it. I am, too.

My sister giggles and, with her mouth half full, mumbles, "You're supposed to eat candy, not read it."

Dr. Lawrence smiles and nods at me. "Well, I guess I can't really argue with that."

The hairstylist turns off the hair dryer and sets it behind me. She fluffs my hair with her hands and then shields my face as she sprays my hair.

The smell of hairspray reminds me of Mother. Of Meryl. Of the women in our community, spraying their fanciest braids and waves, high above their foreheads. I miss them all more than I ever thought I would.

"You ready to take a look?" the stylist asks.

I swallow hard and nod. Cutting my hair seemed like a good idea—another way to become the new me. Now, I'm not so sure.

She spins the chair, and I spot my reflection looking back at me. At least, I think it's me.

The hair I've been growing my entire life—the hair that stretched far below my waist—now barely touches my shoulders. My lip quivers. I press my lips together, feeling the tears sting the backs of my eyes. The hair Mother braided so many times is gone. I don't think she'd even recognize me now.

"Oh no," the stylist says, worry lining her voice. She hands me a tissue. "Maybe we should've cut only a little this time."

I wipe my nose. "It's fine. It's just—"

Dr. Lawrence stands behind me and touches my shoulder reassuringly. "It will take some getting used to, but I like it."

"I think it looks pretty," Amy adds.

I let out a relieved laugh. "You do?"

My sister nods.

"Thank you," I say and blot the corners of my eyes before reexamining my reflection. "Me too."

The stylist gives me a wink. "With that haircut, you're going to be a real heartbreaker at school."

She looks at me in the mirror, as if expecting a response. But I'm not really sure what I'm supposed to say. I shift, uncomfortable as she removes the cape from my neck. It sounded like an insult, but her tone made it sound like a compliment. Just another one of those confusing things here on the outside.

Tanner says I should ask when I'm not sure. "Heartbreaker," I repeat. "Is that a good thing?"

"Oh yeah," the stylist says, shaking the cape. I take one final look in the mirror and nod.

We soon step outside to a brisk, sunny morning in Santa Fe. The familiar Sangre de Cristo Mountains stand watch in the distance. Someone's burning piñon wood in a chiminea on a restaurant patio nearby.

I breathe in the comforting smell as we walk a few doors down the adobe strip mall to meet Tanner and Kel at the coffee shop. A bell jingles as we walk through the door. Wearing T-shirts and jeans, they both grin when they see us.

They look so different now. Especially Kel. He's grown taller, but more than anything, he's more relaxed than I've ever seen him. "Whoa," he says.

Tanner nods, shaking his hand midair. "Look at you two."

Amy spins, showing off her new haircut. People around us stare. I shrink inside my red hoodie.

Tanner laughs at my reaction. "Ready to go?" he asks, tossing a paper cup into a trash bin.

"Where are we going?" I ask Dr. Lawrence.

She adjusts the purse strap on her shoulder. "I need to talk to the private investigator that helped us find Channing's family. I'm going to see if he's gotten any more leads on where your father might be staying." She shakes her head. "Of course, only if that's still what you want me to do?"

I glance at Tanner, who shrugs. He's still angry with Father. And then at Kel and Amy, who both nod. I quickly nod, too. It's time we start trying to bridge that gap.

Dr. Lawrence checks her phone and then suddenly looks up. I can tell she's trying to suppress a smile. "While Kel and I are doing that, Tanner has devised a little errand he wants to run with you."

"What is it?" My gaze darts to her phone, but the screen is already dark.

They all shift around me, acting suspicious. Amy doesn't even try to hide her grin. "We have a surprise for you."

Kel shushes her.

"Don't tell her," Tanner says.

Her jaw goes firm, defiant. "I wasn't going to."

I can't help but smile. I forgot how much I missed their bickering.

"You better get going," Dr. Lawrence says and pushes open the coffee shop's door. The bell jingles, returning us to the scent of burning piñon wood.

I rub my hands together before Amy and I pile into Tanner's rusted orange truck. Once in the driver's seat, my brother rolls down his window.

Dr. Lawrence smiles. "Be back by dinner?"

"Yes, ma'am," Tanner says.

Kel stands behind Dr. Lawrence. "Have fun," he says.

"Oh, we will." Tanner gives them a wink and rolls up the window. They both back away from the truck and wave good-bye as we pull out of the parking lot. The engine roars as we take off.

I nudge Amy, whispering under the noise, "Where are we going?"

"Forget it," Tanner says. "You'll just have to wait and see."

I sigh heavily. Why can't they tell me?

Amy and Tanner look at each other and grin.

We're soon heading south, outside of Santa Fe. My whole

body begins to relax as we drive through the hills of rural New Mexico. I run my fingers through my new haircut as we zoom beneath the expansive blue sky, past the red earth covered with the scrub and sage bushes I associate with home.

The radio blasts unfamiliar songs—one after the other—but Amy bobs and hums with each one like she's known them forever. Tanner taps the steering wheel with the beat. The longer we drive, the songs start to repeat, and I'm sometimes able to join them on the chorus.

After a while, Tanner exits the highway, and we're back in city traffic. This time, it's Albuquerque. My neck tightens with the noise and congestion. "What are we doing here?"

"You'll see," Amy says as Tanner navigates the busy streets. We pass gas stations and restaurants. Offices and shops.

Horns honk. Motors hum. Until my brother maneuvers into the left lane and turns into the parking lot of a two-story reddish-beige building.

My skin tingles as Tanner cuts the engine and jumps from the truck. Amy excitedly pushes me to open the door.

I hop from the truck and look up at the brick and glass and metal building. My heart quickens. A giant decorative metal cutout of a violin clings to the side of the building next to a sign: ROBERTSON AND SONS.

My eyes flash to Tanner. He holds open the door. "Coming?"

With a hurried breath, I enter the two-story lobby with Amy and Tanner on my heels. It smells of wood and rosin and musty paper.

Violin cases line one of the tables to our right. A man in a black apron plays, while another man looks on. A few feet away, a girl plucks the strings on a cello. A woman, who appears to be her mother, nods with approval.

At the end of the carpeted room, a bearded man with white hair and a friendly face greets us. He shakes Tanner's hand. "This must be Gentry," he says, smiling at me.

Tanner points. "And this is my other sister, Amy."

The man claps his hands together. "Well, let's get started."

I want to ask him with what. But, by now, I know they won't answer even if I ask.

We follow the white-haired man down a long hallway and stop at a door. "Let me know if you need anything. Anything at all," he says as he turns to leave. "I'll be in my office."

Tanner opens the door to a large room. There's a stage up front. Black chairs in rows fill the room. It reminds me of our meetinghouse in Watchful.

Up onstage, a girl plays a chestnut-colored violin. She has black hair with blue tips and wears sparkly pink tennis shoes.

A woman sits in one of the chairs, listening. I don't know who the girl is, but she can play. I mean, she can really play. The sound is so rich, I feel like I could cry.

Then, I notice the golden-haired dog at her feet with the red bandanna around his neck. The dog's head pops up from the stage as he seems to notice us, too. He barks; it echoes to the ceiling and back. The girl stops playing and glances over in our direction.

My cheeks flush with embarrassment until she smiles.

"Talia?" I say.

"Gentry!" she squeals and lowers the violin and bow onto the table before running toward me. She slams into me with a hug.

I'm grinning from ear to ear.

When we separate, she nods. "Love the new look."

I point to her blue-tipped hair. "You too."

Rockstar licks Amy's hand. She laughs and pets his shaggy head. Tanner backs away, looking a little wary, and I laugh. "He won't hurt you," I say, and Talia nods with a smile.

I can't believe she's here. That we're all here. "What are you doing here?"

Talia wiggles with excitement. "Mom, you tell her."

Only then do I notice Talia's mom approaching. She must've been the one listening before. She smiles softly. "It's good to see you again, Gentry. Tanner told us about everything you've been through. I'm so sorry."

The back of my neck goes hot.

Talia nudges her mom. "Way to make it awkward, Mom."

"Um, well," Talia's mom says before clearing her throat. "I've been talking to the festival people. We've been collecting money for a worthy cause for almost a year now."

Talia rolls her eyes, looking impatient. "Will you just tell her already?" She shakes her head. "Never mind, I'll do it." She points to the stage. "I've pulled some violins for you to try. If you don't like these, we can pick some more."

My pulse stutters as my gaze jumps to the table on the stage, lined with violins in a range of hues—honey to deep brown. Is she saying what I think she's saying?

Tanner smiles. "Told you she'd like it."

I try to catch my breath. "I can play?"

"You can do a whole lot more than that," Talia says. "When you find one or two you like, you can take them home. Try them out for a while. When you figure out which one you want, the festival will buy it for you."

"On one condition," Talia's mom says, raising a finger.

Talia gives her mom another look. "I was getting to that." She turns to me. "You have to play in the Santa Fe Youth

275

Symphony and agree to take weekly lessons—and play in next summer's festival." Talia cocks her head as she looks at her mother. "That's more than one condition." She shrugs. "Of course, you'll be doing it all with me. *If* that's okay."

I can hardly believe my ears.

Her mom nods at my brother. "Tanner's already agreed to play with you in the festival again next summer."

"Yep." He raises his chin with pride and then adds, "And don't even *think* you'll get to play the lead just because you have a new violin. I'm still the oldest."

I shake my head. "This can't be real."

"I know it's a lot to take in," Talia's mom says.

My body buzzes with possibility. "You *want* me to play?"

She smiles softly. "Of course we do."

"Come on," Talia says, leading me to the stage. Once we climb up, she gestures toward the table. "Which one do you want to try first?"

I immediately grab the chestnut violin she was playing and place it under my chin.

She nods with approval. "Good choice."

The wood still feels warm in my hand.

They settle in the front row; Rockstar plops at Amy's feet. She strokes his golden head and side over and over, whispering, "Good dog."

I pick a bow from the table and glance over the scroll at Tanner. "What should I play?"

My brother shakes his head with a smile. "This time, you choose."

With a grin, I touch my bow to the string. Then, I play "Red-Haired Boy." Within a few measures, the music takes over. Like it always has. It runs through me. I feel free.

As I play, I think of Father. Mother. My whole family. Some in Watchful. Some in Waiting. And some out here with me. Then, I think of Channing. And the new friends I've made.

When I finish playing, everyone jumps and cheers. Talia whistles. Rockstar wags his fluffy tail; it smacks against Amy's leg, making her laugh.

I bow, grateful. I don't have to think about the end of the world anymore.

Now, I'm only looking forward to the beginning.

Acknowledgments

First off, thank you so much to Sonali Fry for trusting me to tell this story. Your support and enthusiasm have made my debut experience better than I could have ever imagined. Thank you also to Gayley Avery, Nadia Almahdi, Lauren Carr, and Crystal McCoy for fielding my approximately one billion questions with patience and grace. You are the best! Also, thank you to Colleen Tighe for your beautiful cover art, to David DeWitt for your fantastic design, and to the entire Yellow Jacket team for loving Gentry's story.

Thank you to Rick Richter for believing in my writing. I'm so grateful for your invaluable acumen, determination, and experience.

I want to extend a heartfelt thanks to J. Suzanne Frank, writing instructor and community creator extraordinaire, for your faith in my early work, for always welcoming me back into the Writer's Path community, and for listening.

Thank you also to Daniel J. Hale, master plot instructor and ceaseless cheerleader, for saying I had the "moxie" to tell the stories I wanted to tell and for all of your encouragement, advice, and wit.

Hema Penmetsa, thank you for sharing New York with me seven years ago when all we had was a manuscript and a dream.

I'm so glad I experienced that time with you, and I'm incredibly grateful we get to continue this journey together. Thank you also for inviting me to join the best critique group ever. Hema, Polly Holyoke, Pam McWilliams, and Robert Eilers: Thank you for your brutal honesty, your beautiful writing, and most of all, the laughs. You all are awesome!

Several Dallas-area children's writers also deserve my many thanks, especially Laney Nielson, Karen Harrington, Karen Blumenthal, and Marci Peschke, who have welcomed me into this community with open arms. Thank you for your advice and support and making this debut journey a whole lot more fun.

Years ago, I took my first religious studies course in college. Little did I know then that the spark of curiosity had ignited a fire in me that would feed a lifetime of wanting to learn more. Thank you to Dr. Richard Cogley, that first instructor and my college mentor, and to the Religious Studies Department at SMU for your collective wisdom and passion for your field.

To my mom, thank you for expressing your love of books from as far back as I can remember. I'm so grateful you also encouraged determination (though some may say "stubbornness") in me, while always demonstrating the importance of compassion for others.

Thank you to my amazing Madeline for believing in me.

You were the first person to read Gentry's words, and she is a better character because of you. Thank you for asking me each day how the writing was going. I'm so blessed by your insight, honesty, intellect, humor, and love.

Last, but definitely not least, I am so grateful to you, Shane. Even when I first expressed an interest in writing (but didn't have a clue as to how to start), you told me you'd love to read my work. And at times when I felt like I might give up, you told me I couldn't. Thank you for supporting me always, believing in me always, and loving me always. I'm so fortunate I get to share this life with you.